THE LEGACY SERIES

SERIES TITLES

The Correct Response
Manfred Gabriel

The Three Devils and Other Stories
William Luvaas

Welcome Back to the World: A Novella & Stories
Rob Davidson

Greyhound Cowboy and Other Stories
Ken Post

Close Call
Kim Suhr

The Waterman
Gary Schanbacher

Signs of the Imminent Apocalypse and Other Stories
Heidi Bell

What We Might Become
Sara Reish Desmond

The Silver State Stories
Michael Darcher

An Instinct for Movement
Michael Mattes

The Machine We Trust
Tim Conrad

Gridlock
Brett Biebel

THE CORRECT RESPONSE

STORIES

MANFRED GABRIEL

CORNERSTONE PRESS
UNIVERSITY OF WISCONSIN-STEVENS POINT

Cornerstone Press, Stevens Point, Wisconsin 54481
Copyright © 2025 Manfred Gabriel
www.uwsp.edu/cornerstone

Printed in the United States of America by
Point Print and Design Studio, Stevens Point, Wisconsin

Library of Congress Control Number: 2024948516
ISBN: 978-1-960329-52-3

Cornerstone Press titles are produced in courses and internships offered by the Department of English at the University of Wisconsin–Stevens Point.

DIRECTOR & PUBLISHER
Dr. Ross K. Tangedal

EXECUTIVE EDITORS
Jeff Snowbarger, Freesia McKee

EDITORIAL DIRECTOR
Ellie Atkinson

SENIOR EDITORS
Brett Hill, Grace Dahl

PRESS STAFF
Sam Bjork, Madalyn Carpenter, Mai Kao Hang, Karlie Harpold, Allison Lange, Sophie McPherson, Kylie Newton, Christiana Niedzwiecki, Hannah Rouer, Holly White, Ava Willett

To my children, Lily-Ann, Ari, and Marie.
Three of the greatest blessings any father could ever ask for.

STORIES

The Fae Sing

Christina watched Belinda from her own front yard for a long while before crossing the street to say hello. Belinda sat with her legs tucked under her, drawing with sidewalk chalk. She appeared lost in her slow, deliberate strokes, not seeming to notice Christina as she approached.

"What are you making?" Christina asked. She towered over Belinda with legs apart and arms crossed, the sun behind her, her face in shadow.

Belinda squinted at Christina, pushed her dark-framed glasses up on her nose. She had a thick piece of pink chalk in her hand. A three-by-three section of sidewalk was laid out in front of her like a canvas. There was a rainbow, a bright orange sun. A bluebird flew across the sky.

Christina knew it was a dumb question. Belinda must have thought so as well. She went back to her artwork without responding.

"My mom said I should come say hi to you. You being new and everything," Christina continued. The "For Sale - Sold" sign still stood in the front yard of Belinda's house—a pale green story-and-a-half with white trim. "Not that I need any more friends or anything."

Christina glanced around, hoping no one from school saw her talking to this new girl who still colored on sidewalks like some kindergartener. When Belinda didn't answer right away, Christina saw her chance to slip away, go back and tell her mother she had done her neighborly duty. She started to turn when Belinda said, "Ever seen a fairy?" She spoke without looking up, busy using the pink chalk to color a long-eared bunny.

"I'm too old to believe in fairies," Christina replied. Her mother had spoken with Belinda and her mother the day before, when the family first arrived. She went on about how nice they were and told her Belinda was going into fifth grade, too. They might even have the same teacher next year. Christina thought Belinda was too small to be her own age. If she was going to go around school talking about fairies, well, the last thing Christina needed was to be associated with something so childish. Not when other girls were already getting cell phones and wearing training bras.

"Do you believe in rabbits?" Belinda asked.

Christina didn't know how to respond. She scratched her head.

Belinda stopped drawing, leaned back, inspected her work. She pulled her stringy black hair back behind her ear. "You've seen rabbits. Petted one, no doubt. Who knows, you might've even eaten one." She scrunched up her face.

She had a tiny nose, almost like a rabbit's, Christina thought.

"If someone asked if you've ever seen one, you wouldn't say you don't believe in them. Belief has nothing to do with it."

"But I've seen rabbits," Christina said. "I've never seen a fairy." Belinda stood up, brushed the chalk from her hands onto her faded denim shorts. She smiled. "Would you like to?"

A FEW MINUTES LATER, they were standing in Belinda's backyard in front of the fence that divided her and Harrison's house. The fence was easily twice their height, made of wide cedar panels laid close together so that there wasn't even the smallest gap between them. It stretched all around the backyard like some medieval fortress wall. Behind the fence rose several tall trees—oaks and walnuts and maples. Their leaves lush and green.

"I was up in my room yesterday," Belinda said, pointing to the dormer that faced Harrison's yard. "You can't see into his yard from there. The tree branches are too thick. But then I noticed the leaves moving back and forth. It didn't seem natural. It wasn't the wind. It wasn't a squirrel or a bird. I have a window seat and a place for books. I sat and watched those trees for an hour or so, then I saw it. It flitted by so fast. It was there and then gone."

"It was probably a butterfly or moth," Christina said.

Belinda shook her head. "I know what I saw. This morning, I went and tried the gate to get a closer look, but it was locked."

"Harrison likes his privacy," Christina confirmed. Harrison was an older man. He lived in the house alone. He never went to block parties. He never showed up at the annual Fourth of July parade. People only saw him for brief moments—getting out of his car after work, taking out the garbage Wednesday evenings, mowing his front lawn every Saturday. Christina wasn't even sure if Harrison was his first or last name.

Christina wondered what kind of girl Belinda was, willing to go into a stranger's yard after who knows what. Brave, naïve, or stupid, she couldn't be sure. Already, Christina knew she and Belinda could never be friends. The other girls would never accept Belinda. She could never fit in. And more than anything, Christina *wanted* to fit in—wear the same clothes, listen to the same music, feign the same sudden interest in boys. Still, she couldn't help but be curious. It wasn't that long ago that she lost her last teeth, finding a dollar in its place under the pillow the next morning. Even though she knew it was her mother who put it there.

"So how we going to get in?" Christina asked, not wanting to sound less daring than her new neighbor.

Belinda went into her garage. Through the open side door, Christina could see boxes from the move still waiting to be unpacked. She heard Belinda rummaging around. Belinda reemerged holding a jump rope in one hand, a hammer in the other. The jump rope was long; the kind that two people needed to twirl while one or more skipped in between. Belinda tied one end around the hammer's handle in a clumsy knot. She threw it up and into Harrison's trees. It went through the branches that hung over Belinda's yard and fell with a thud, almost hitting Christina's foot. She jumped back, "Hey! Are you crazy?"

Belinda shrugged. She picked up the hammer and threw it again. This time, it caught tight in the tree's boughs. She tugged at it, checking if it would hold her weight. She handed the other end of the rope to Christina.

Christina took another step back. "You first."

Belinda started up the rope, bracing her feet against the fence. Hand over hand, she clambered to the top. She struggled to straddle it, her hair hanging over her face. Belinda let herself drop to the other side. Christina heard a thud. For a moment, she thought Belinda might have fallen on her head, lying unconscious. Finally, Christina heard her voice. "What are you waiting for?" she said. "You chicken?"

Christina pulled her blond hair back into a ponytail, tied it with a hair tie she kept in her pocket. She'd have to get it cut again before school started. All the girls were wearing their hair short this year. She took the rope in her hands, curled her toes so that her flip-flops wouldn't fall off her feet, and began to climb.

At the top of the fence, she found a netting so thin it was almost invisible ran between the trees, twisted around their branches, forming a mesh roof over the entire yard. Christina squeezed through a small gap where the netting met the fence and let herself drop, hitting her knee as she landed.

"It's like a forest," Belinda said.

Christina sat on the ground, rubbing her knee. Slivers of filtered sunlight shined between the trees. There was no lawn. Instead, woodchips covered the ground. A stone path led from the house's back deck to the gate. Ivy grew up the inside of the fence. Wildflowers sprang up here and there. Moss clung to the grey bark of the trees. Mushrooms flourished at their roots.

"So, where are the fairies?" Christina asked, doubt in her voice.

Belinda walked up to a plant that grew almost as tall as she was. Blue flowers, like tiny bells, hung from its stem. She bent towards it, breathed deep. "If they were easy to spot, everyone would believe in them."

"You must not have had many friends where you lived."

"If you don't like my apples …"

Christina gave Belinda a quizzical look. "Mom said there were things people around here wouldn't understand."

Belinda shook her head and laughed. Christina never liked being laughed at. It reminded her of the girls at school. The ones she wanted to be friends with, always whispering to each other in the hall, giggling as Christina passed.

Christina leaped up, shoved Belinda with both hands. Belinda's back cracked against a tree. She rushed at Christina, and they both fell over. They rolled around in the woodchips, scratching and clawing at each other. Christina ended up on top of Belinda, her knees pinning the girl down at the shoulders. She paused, unsure of what to do next. Belinda struggled but was unable to break free.

She stopped struggling. Christina thought she had given up. Then, out of the corner of her eye, she caught a glimpse of something flitting at the side of her head. Suddenly, it flew in front of her face, its wings blinding her. Christina swatted at it, then fell backward. Belinda sat up. They both stared for a long while as it flew in circles around them. It was only about six inches tall with a round, featureless face and bulbous eyes that seemed to be all pupils—no whites, no irises. It had a fat little belly, chubby arms and legs. It was completely naked and hairless. They could not tell if it was male or female.

"Not what I expected," Christina said finally.

"Disney had it all wrong," Belinda agreed.

It flew down, took Christina's hand, held it out. Then it did the same to Belinda, moving her hand so that the girls' fingertips almost touched. The girls, bewildered, did not resist. "I think it wants us to shake hands," Belinda said.

Reluctantly, the girls shook each other's hands, palms both soaked in sweat, barely touching. The fairy landed on the ground. Its wings kept moving. It groaned, a loud and low-pitched noise made without ever opening its mouth.

"I think it's coming from its wings," Belinda said.

Other fairies began to appear from tree knolls and flower blossoms and the boughs of the trees. Some seemed to come out of nowhere, appearing suddenly in mid-air. They flew around the two girls like so many fireflies on a mid-summer evening. Each looked slightly different. Some were thinner, some fatter. A few had long, stringy hair. A few were only half the size of the others. Whether these were children or not was impossible to tell.

As if on cue, they began to sing with the flapping of their wings. But they were not singing as one. They were not in harmony. It was hard for the girls to tell whether they were singing the same song at all. Some voices were low, like the fairy who had first appeared. Some were high-pitched falsettos. As the girls listened, at first it seemed to them to be nothing but noise, but as it continued, it seemed that they could pick out individuals. Each one beautiful in its own way. Together, the girls realized that this singing was language, and they knew what the fairies were trying to say.

They were saying hello.

AFTER WHAT SEEMED LIKE AN ENDLESS TIME, the singing dwindled and stopped. The girls sat on the ground, hair covered in woodchips, faces dirty. Christina's knee didn't hurt so much anymore. Some of the fairies were sitting on the ground, watching them with their round, dark eyes. Others flitted here and there, seeming to take no notice of them, on some personal business all their own. Belinda tried to count them, but they flew too fast for her to know whether or not she was counting some twice. She gave up at thirty-three.

"So, this why old Harrison always keeps his gate locked," Christina said.

Belinda looked up at the trees. "They can't seem to get through the netting. I think he's keeping them here."

"I went to the conservatory once," Christina said. "It had a butterfly garden beneath a large tent made like this. Those butterflies couldn't get away either. Prisoners."

Belinda paused. "So how do we set them free?" Christina was about to tell Belinda she was crazy for the second time that day when they heard a loud, rumbling sound out front. Harrison's truck was pulling onto the drive. It was then they both realized that their way of getting into the yard didn't allow them to get out again. They looked at each other with panicked faces. They heard footsteps coming toward the gate. Harrison was undoing the lock. The fairies scattered. None could be seen. Christina glanced around. The deck, they could hide beneath it. Belinda seemed paralyzed with fear. Christina took her hand and practically dragged her along. They scrambled beneath the deck just as Harrison entered the yard.

The deck was only a couple of feet off the ground. They had to lie flat between the piers. Christina lifted her head slightly and peered out, but all she could see were Harrison's work boots, splattered with dirt and drops of paint. He stood in the middle of the yard and started to make a noise, as close to the song the fairies made as was possible for a human voice.

Christina felt something pulling on the leg of her shorts. It was Belinda. She was nearer to the house, looking through a small window into Harrison's basement. She had it partway open, was already slipping inside. Christina thought this was a bad idea, but she didn't dare say anything for fear Harrison would hear her. Instead, she crawled to the window just as Belinda made her way in. Being bigger than Belinda, it was a tight fit, but she managed to squeak through.

The basement was unfinished, the cement block walls crammed with shelves. In the far corner stood a washer, dryer, utility sink, and pile of dirty clothes. On the wall nearby sat several dozen mason jars. Their caps were off and scattered about, holes punched into them. In one of the jars, there came the tiniest spark of light. The two girls approached, peered inside. There was a wing. A fairy wing.

"He locks them up in these jars," Belinda whispered. "Tortures them, no doubt."

"I didn't notice any missing a wing," Christina replied.

"Probably tortured it to death," Belinda said. "Ate it, most likely."

They could still hear Harrison singing through the open window. Christina nodded at the wooden staircase leading up. "Let's get out of here. We can head through the front door while he's still out back."

They hurried up the stairs, running out the front door without looking back.

"WE HAVE TO HELP THEM," Belinda said. They were in her backyard. They could not hear the fairies singing any longer. Earlier, they heard the back door shut. Presumably, Harrison had gone inside.

"How are we going to do that?" Christina asked. They lay on the grass, their hearts beating fast from the fear of almost being caught.

"We could call the police."

"And tell them what, that we saw fairies? I don't think they have any laws about fairy abuse, even if they did believe us. Probably get in trouble for trespassing."

They felt the coming and going of the sun's warm light as it peaked in and out of passing white clouds.

"How about cutting the mesh?" Belinda asked after a time.

"How about minding your own business?" a man's voice said from behind them.

Christina and Belinda turned. Harrison stood a few feet away. They sat up and looked at each other, both thinking the same thing: *run, he can't catch us both*. But then what? He knew who they were, where they lived. The next step would be to go to their parents. Then they'd be in even more trouble, sneaking into a neighbor's yard.

"You forgot your hammer," Harrison said, dropping it on the ground.

Christina started to speak. "We were just—"

"You don't need to apologize," Belinda interrupted. "He's the monster."

Christina was amazed and a bit in awe of Belinda's bravery. He could get them in big trouble, and here she was calling him names.

Harrison was a tall, lean man. He had a couple of day's growth of beard, much grayer than his salt and pepper crew cut. He had a puzzled look on his face, as if he didn't understand what Belinda was talking about.

"You keep them. Like animals," Belinda said.

Harrison laughed. "I don't keep them. They can leave any time they want. The netting isn't that tight, and they aren't stupid. Even you got through it."

"But then why is it there?" Christina asked.

Harrison sat down on the ground. "I bought the house five years ago. You weren't here, and you weren't old enough to remember," He nodded at Belinda and Christina in turn. "Old lady used to own it. You think *I'm* a recluse? No one ever even saw her come or go. Real witch. Died in that house. Anyway, I bought the house sight unseen. I was moving in from another town for work. Only saw pictures. Market was hot then. Had to make an offer before anyone even had a chance to take a look. When I moved in, there was some stuff left behind—an old door that used to hang in the kitchen, some paint cans of god-awful pink and baby blue that were used in the bedrooms, and those mason jars you must have seen. Each one sealed, each one containing a tiny person."

"*Fairy*," Belinda corrected him.

Harrison thought a moment. "Guess they are. Anyway, they looked like fireflies all cooped up like that, so I let them out. Never could stand to see living things suffer. I expected them to fly away, but instead, they made a home out of my backyard."

"But what about the netting?" Christina asked.

"I'm getting to that," Harrison said. "I liked watching them from my kitchen. One Saturday afternoon, I'm watching them and what do I see but a hawk come down, snatch one right out of the air."

"A hawk?" Christina said.

Harrison nodded. "They live along the lake about a mile from here. Hunt fish mostly, but this one found easier pickings. Got two more before the rest went into hiding. All that was left was a single wing. That's when I put up the netting. Just finished fixing the gap you made. Fortunately, nothing more than a couple of nosy girls got through."

Belinda smiled. "The netting's not to keep them in, it's to keep predators out?"

Harrison nodded again. "If you want to tell on me, go ahead. But others will come, scientists, probably, and take them to some university for experiments. Or the media, with their cameras. Then they'll never have any peace."

"We won't tell if you won't," Christina said, holding out her hand.

Harrison shook it. "Deal." He got up, started out, stopped suddenly. "One thing. I hate to admit needing advice from a couple of kids, but I have to know. Did they come to you?"

"Yes," Belinda said.

"They've never come to me," Harrison said. "Even though I've learned their song. They hide whenever they see me, like that one that peaked up over the fence. Just once, I wish they'd come to me, wish they knew I was their friend."

He left, his head low. After he was gone, the girls sat silently for a while. After a time, they heard him singing again. Finally, Belinda rose. "I think I know why the fairies came to us and not him. Come on."

The two girls found the gate shut, but Harrison had left his front door unlocked. They ran through it to the backyard. He stood on his deck, facing away from them. No fairies could be seen.

They ran at him, grabbing his legs. He shouted in surprise, falling over. They both sat on him and started hitting him. He pushed at them, not as hard as he could, obviously not wanting to hurt them. He asked over and over what was going on.

At least a dozen fairies appeared as if from nowhere. They flew at the girls, getting in their faces, flying between their hands and Harrison's body to keep them from hitting him again. The girls stopped, got off of Harrison, letting him stand. The fairies remained.

"I don't understand," Harrison said.

Belinda spoke, "When the first fairy came to us, we were fighting. I figured that's what must have brought them out. They don't like violence."

Harrison chuckled. "And all this time, I thought I needed to be nice."

The fairies were pushing at the girls' backs now, shoving them towards Harrison. Both they and the man understood. They gave each other big hugs. The fairies joined hands in a large ring around their heads, began to spin in a circle. Harrison released the girls and tilted his head up, watching, eyes wide.

Belinda motioned to Christina that it was time to go. They went back out through the house. They found themselves on the sidewalk again, near where Belinda had been making her chalk drawing. Christina inspected it for a few moments, then said, "I think it's missing something." She knelt down, picked up one of the pieces of chalk Belinda had left there, started drawing one of the fairies beneath the rainbow's arc. It looked similar to the first one they saw, round and winged and not at all fairy-like.

Cars passed. Other kids biked by on the other side of the street. Christina went right on drawing. She didn't care who saw.

Old Rocker

The rocking chair arrived via a local delivery service. The driver had Garret sign for it on a tablet with his finger after taking it out of the truck and setting it in the middle of the already crowded living room. Garret considered his birthday gift for a few moments before moving it near the front window, open to a summer breeze.

"Where'd that come from?" Tanya asked her father when she arrived that evening for his annual birthday dinner. She made a face that told Garret she didn't approve. He wasn't surprised. Its dark wood was worn away at the arms. The green chair pad was frayed as if by cat claws and had what looked like a large coffee stain in the middle. Dings and dents marred its legs and runners. Tanya lived about an hour away, in a tidy condo where nothing was ever out of place and all the furniture looked like it had just come off the showroom floor.

"I have no idea," Garret said. "There was no note. I asked the delivery man, but he didn't seem to know much English."

"You should call the company on Monday and ask. Maybe send it back."

Garret laughed. "No way." The chair creaked as he settled into it. He could feel the hard wood seat through the worn cushion. "An old rocker for an old rocker. Get it?"

Tanya shook her head. Her father had made his living in studios and on stage, playing guitar for the Rolling Stones; Crosby, Stills, Nash & Young; Eric Clapton, and a hundred others long forgotten. He'd still be playing now if arthritis hadn't made it hard to lift a coffee mug, let alone strum a Gibson.

His daughter sighed, "Where do you want to go to eat?"

"Where do you think?" he said.

"Come on Dad, don't you want to go somewhere nice?"

"I'm the one turning seventy today. It's nice enough for me."

TANYA INSISTED ON DRIVING. Iggy's Diner sat next to a gas station on Route 50. The gas station used to be a butcher shop, and before that a flower shop. Even though it had changed owners several times, Iggy's had always been Iggy's, with its gray cement block walls and red tin roof. It no longer had a drive-in, too expensive to pay carhops, and no one wanted to sit in their parked car and eat anyway, but it still had an outside order window and plastic picnic tables. You could eat inside at booths with vinyl benches, if you didn't mind the sticky floors and the charred meat smell that drifted from a grill slick with years of beef fat.

It was unseasonably cool for August, so they decided to eat outside, to Tanya's apparent relief. "At least I won't have to peel the grease from the bottom of my shoes when I get home," she said.

They placed their orders at the window with a kid who didn't look old enough to be out of high school, then waited under the eave for their number to be called. Several other people stood with them, college students, mostly, on their phones. The nearby university's semester didn't start for another couple of days, but underclassmen had already started to make their way into town. Now and then, one of the professors from the music department would reach out to Garret, asking him to guest lecture. He was no teacher, so these talks usually consisted of him regaling students with stories of the good old days. While he was talking, he often felt invigorated from being around music majors who knew their history well enough to be aware of even some of the more esoteric people he was talking about, often asking intriguing questions. Afterwards, though, he felt a bit sad and in need of a drink—to mourn the loss of many of those he'd played with, to mourn his *own* inability to play anymore.

Both Garret's parents loved classical music but had almost no talent. They started Garret with violin lessons when he was six years old. He played like a natural. They were almost despondent when he switched to guitar at the age of twelve. Not just any guitar, but electric guitar. He could appreciate Bach and Brahms, Vivaldi and Paganini, but he had no passion for them. He wanted to emulate the music he heard on the radio and on the 45s he bought at the nearby record store, modern virtuosos like Hendrix and Santana and Paige. He never got to be a star, of course, but he built a modest career not only playing the music he loved but recording ad jingles and TV theme songs. That time was long gone. Now, everything was digitized, and real music played by real musicians had little value.

Garret and Tanya's order was ready. They brought their food to the nearest picnic table. Garret took a large bite of a triple bacon burger, shoving an onion ring into his mouth before he even swallowed.

"You won't live to seventy-one, eating like that," Tanya said.

"Okay, *Mom*," he replied, wiping mustard from his stubbled chin. "Maybe you should try it. Look at those fries. You don't even have any cheese on them."

Tanya frowned at her basket. Plain fries and a Diet Coke were all she ordered. She was tall and skinny, so much so that people often thought she had an eating disorder, but one look at her mother, who now lived happily on the East

Coast with a new husband, and it was obvious it was all in the genes.

"At least I'm here," Tanya said.

Garret nodded at that. Tanya had always been there, even when she was a little girl. Making sure he got up and was washed and dressed for his gigs. She'd throw his vomit-soaked sheets in the wash. She'd call and make excuses for him when he was too drunk to work.

"I miss your sister too," Garret replied.

They ate in silence after that, cars zipping past, more students coming and going, a few families ordering Iggy's famous homemade ice cream. Garret took the last bite of his burger. The summer was coming to an end, and the sun was just above the trees. "We should probably go back," he said.

Tanya shrugged. She finished her Diet Coke, but her fries remained half-eaten. She tossed them into an overflowing garbage can as they got back into her car.

"Thanks for taking me out for my birthday," Garret said as they pulled up to the curb in front of his house.

"I'll see you sometime," Tanya replied, hands still on the wheel, eyes fixed straight ahead.

The porch light came on as he approached the front door, courtesy of a motion detector Tanya had him install a few years back. Inside, the living room was gray with the dying light. He went to switch on a lamp when he heard his new old rocker creaking and saw Mo sitting there. He could barely make out her face in the dwindling light, blue eyes that had lost their twinkle, a dimple hidden in a face that had aged too quickly. She wore plaid pants with black boots and a corduroy jacket over a flannel shirt, much too warm even for this unseasonably cool weather. She had cut her hair short since the last time Garret had seen her. He liked it that way.

"Happy birthday, Old Man."

He smiled at that. She always called him Old Man, even when she was a little girl, and he was still young.

"You should say hi to your sister," Garret said. Tanya's car still sat on the curb; her silhouette visible in the driver's seat.

Mo frowned. She ran a hand across the arm of the chair. "I see my gift arrived."

Garret asked Mo if she wanted something to drink. She asked for water, with lots of ice. He went to the kitchen and got the water for her, pulling out a non-alcoholic beer for himself. His sponsor told him more than once that it wasn't a good idea, that it still had a small amount of alcohol. He didn't care. He liked the taste even if it wasn't the real stuff. As for the program, he didn't think much of all the God mumbo-jumbo, even with Mo in the next room as non-living proof that there must be more beyond this life. Still, daily meetings provided a place to be with people like himself, people who understood, and it kept him sober for one more day.

He may not have cared what his sponsor thought, but he cared about what Mo thought. He wondered what she might say if he returned with a beer, real or not. He put the bottle back into the fridge, pouring himself some water instead, no ice. When he returned to the living room, she took the glass from him and drank half of it in one swallow.

"Must be hot down there," he said.

"They don't send you to hell for being sick. It's not heaven, either. More like rehab for the dead." She finished her water and held the empty glass up to him. He went to refill it.

"You're not just here for the chair, or water," Garret said when he returned. "If there's any way I can help you—"

She held up her hand. "Too late for me. Don't worry, I've long since forgiven you. They have this strange form of therapy. Forces you to look deep inside. More anguish than pits of fire or being buried in lava up to your neck. Still, I came out of it, realized it wasn't your fault."

A hole formed in Garret's stomach. No matter what she said, he knew if he had just been a better father it would have made all the difference. He could not save her, but she had saved him. That night in the emergency room, after the doctor had given him the news, he swore off drinking for good. He had the feeling that she was here to help him again, although he didn't see how. He sat on the couch and set his own water on the table next to him. "If you're not here for yourself then why are you here?"

She continued rocking, looking out the window. Tanya hadn't left yet. She sat in the driver's seat, unmoving, her head hung low. "She acts like she has it all together. She doesn't. She misses you."

"I spend as much time with her as I can," he replied.

"Time is not what she's looking for. You still have that old guitar you used to play when we were little?"

"My playing days are over." He held up his hand to display slightly bulging knuckles and a bent pinkie finger.

"It's supposed to hurt."

He didn't know how to respond to that. She stared at him until he finally got up and went down the hall to the extra bedroom that doubled as a music room. There were a couple of amps, an electronic keyboard he never learned to play well, and several guitars—a Gibson 335 and a Fender Telecaster among them, gathering dust. Tanya tried to convince him to sell the lot. "You could use the money and they aren't doing you any good here," she had said. He'd agree just to appease her but knew he could never bring himself to part with them.

The guitar Mo referred to was a Martin D12-35 12-String acoustic. It hung on the wall above a sagging sleeper sofa. He took it down, stopped, then chose an appropriate pick from a collection in an old ashtray on the dresser. He returned to the living room. Mo was gone. His heart sank. He looked out the window to see Tanya still sitting there, the orange glow of a cigarette near her lips. It took him aback. He hadn't seen her smoke since she was a teenager.

He sat in the rocker, the guitar on his knee. He played a few chords, struggling to get his fingering just right, wincing with pain, not only from arthritis but from the sound of the instrument, horribly out of tune from misuse and the humidity of summer. He took some time to retune it by ear. At least he still had his hearing.

He plucked the strings, something like a song but completely made up. His fingers felt as if they were on fire. He played slowly, making sure he got the notes right, moving from one to another in the most efficient way possible to numb the pain.

When Tanya and Mo were young, he used to play for them at bedtime, sober or not. It wasn't until they got older that they noticed the difference. His absent-minded playing soon developed into one of the songs they liked most. A song simple and sweet that helped them drift off to sleep.

Garret could no longer recall the name of the song. He found himself becoming more forgetful as the years went by. Whether from age or all the alcohol, he had no way of knowing. His fingers remembered it, though. A song not suitable for radio because it had no lyrics, and yet it spoke to him all the same.

The music drifted out the window. A couple walking their dog stopped to listen and then moved on. He continued to play, keeping one eye on Tanya's car. She still did not move. He wondered if she could hear him through closed car windows. He thought of playing louder, but that would ruin the tone of the song, strip it of its emotion, like light rain in spring. He considered going outside to play on his front step, but he realized he needed to be in this chair. It somehow allowed him to play again.

Finally, Tanya rolled down her passenger side window. She lifted her head, turning towards the house. Garret kept playing. She got out of the car and started walking towards him. Garret's fingers still ached, a dull pain, manageable, but impossible to ignore.

Panel by Panel

"My life is a graphic novel—all straight lines and subtle curves, white space and shadows and shades of black. I speak in bold block lettering. I think in italics. Each moment is a separate frame. Snapshots of life unfolding one-by-one, strung together to resemble a continuous whole."

I am alone on the page. My face is slightly off-center. My eyes are too big for my skeletal face. My ghostly skin is framed by darkness. Each sentence I speak is an individual box running down the right-hand side, one right after the other.

"So, you're some sort of superhero," she says. A new frame shows the two of us sitting together on a bar bench. The smirk on her face is one of humored disbelief.

I shake my head, a few arced lines on either side to denote movement. "Not one of those glossies in the chain bookstores," I say. "Not Green Lantern or Spiderman. I'm not put out by DC or Marvel. A few cheap pages stapled together to be read casually and tossed in a box, stored in the crawl space or attic until they yellow and fall apart. My life isn't in color. It's drawn by some artist living in a basement apartment, white pencil and ink put to black paper in the late hours of the night under bright lamplight. Printed by some publisher no one has heard of, shelved spine out amongst so many other alternative presses in neighborhood shops with worn carpeting and plywood bookcases."

She sips her wine, looks down at the floor. Her eyes are pointed at the corners with black eyeliner, giving her the slightly Asian, slightly sad appearance that's in fashion these days. We sit in a private room in the back of a club I happened on by chance, looking for somewhere to hide. It was loud with a techno-beat. The floors and bars and tiny round tables were slick with sweat. Strobes bouncing off mirrors blinded me. I stayed longer than I wanted, nursing a beer, constantly checking the faceless crowd that had formed a ring around me. I could get lost in here, I thought, a thought bubble floating overhead.

She still has that doubting look, lips down-turned, gaze evasive.

"You think I'm crazy, or drunk," I say.

"It doesn't matter," she replies. It was she who approached me, led me by the hand to this little room, sat me down next to her on this faux leather couch, and stroked my thigh while we talked.

"It matters to me," I say. The floor is carpeted, a deep shag. One corner is turned up slightly. Dog-eared.

I point to it. "There, pull on that."

She shrugs, sets her empty wine glass on the floor, twisting it down so it stays flat on the thick pile. She strides to where the carpet is coming up. She wears boots to her knees, a short suede skirt. On her bare shoulder, just above her halter top, is a tattoo in the shape of a gothic cross. I lean back. I enjoy watching her walk. She's not model-pretty, but she's sexy. It's all in the clothes, the makeup, the attitude. She bends at the waist, no doubt for my benefit, picks up the corner of carpet. She pulls on it hesitantly. It seems stuck tight to the floor.

"Give it a good yank," I say.

She takes the carpet in both hands. The muscles in her slender arms flex as she begins to lift it. She pulls a good three feet of carpeting off the floor. There is a slight tearing sound as she rips it up. She looks at me.

"All the way," I say.

She straightens, pulling the carpet over her head. It folds down on top of her and…

Her and I, on the bar bench, kissing, mouths slightly parted, our heads taking up the entire page, our faces stark, the only color the merlot red of her lips. Our eyes are closed, my lashes are almost non-existent, hers are like the feathers of some exotic bird. The room is shades of black, except for the open doorway in the corner. We do not notice the man standing there, long as a morning shadow, his face white and expressionless, his pose one of a cat prepared to pounce.

SHE TELLS ME HER APARTMENT ISN'T FAR. We walk along a deserted street. Discarded newspapers and shopping bags whipped up by the wind collect in the gutters. It creates a rustling sound, the turning of pages. The street is dark. We are locked in a wedge of light from a streetlamp overhead, our legs caught in mid-step. Cars parked on the curbs are all late model, sedans and SUVs and hatchbacks of no remarkable make. The buildings drawn on either side of us only hint at detail, a few bricks in a wall, a curtained window, a gated storefront.

"I don't understand," she says.

I try to explain, "Some people live in soap operas, every event a crisis. Others live in broad farcical plays, filled with pratfalls and crass jokes. Most live in television reruns, their lives one long routine. Each day is the same as the next."

"Has it always been this way?" she asks.

"Not always," I reply. "You create the life you lead."

She leans in close to me, her head on my shoulder, her hand in mine, tucked deep into my overcoat pocket. Before we left the club, she put on a short leather jacket without a lining. Her legs are bare from knee to thigh. I can feel her body shaking in the cold night air.

"Do you want to wear my coat?" I ask.

"I thought chivalry was dead," she replies.

Our bodies fill the frame. We stop walking and are standing on the sidewalk. My overcoat is in my hands, open to her like wings unfurled. My sweater's sleeves come down around my palms. She turns her back to me. I drape the coat over her shoulders. She wraps it around herself, and as she does, my butterfly knife slips from the inside pocket.

Another panel. This time a close-up: the knife on the cold white sidewalk, the blade tucked into its brushed metallic handle.

"I forgot it was there," I say, snatching it up.

Her blood-red lips tremble. I doubt it is from the cold.

"This world I live in, it isn't always safe." I look around. A cab without a passenger passes by. Other than that, we are alone. "I'll ditch it if you want," I tell her.

She holds out her palm. In the last frame of the page, I place the knife in her hand.

THE ALLEY IS A CAVE WITHOUT END. "A shortcut," she says. Our boots click-clack against the worn pavement. I hear the scurrying of rats—tiny footsteps, claws on concrete—moving quickly. More pages turn.

My eyes have become accustomed to the night. The white strokes on the black page are lighter than before. There are yards of dirt, parking spots of gravel, garages with graffitied doors, wooden porches with winding steps. Like the street, none of this is fully detailed, as if the artist couldn't be bothered with anything that didn't move the story along. They are abstractions. We are ghosts, walking through some never-world.

From behind a fence a dog barks, loud and piercing. A lady yells at it to be quiet, but it does not stop. We come to a spot where two apartment buildings share a common outer wall. A set of cracked stairs leads to a tunnel that runs beneath them to the next street. She starts to lead me down them, but I hesitate. Traps lie everywhere. In simple, angled lettering that denotes my thoughts, I wonder whether or not she is part of a plot to ensnare me.

Extreme close-up: her face is turned so that the left half fills the frame. One eye is angled towards me, her nose sloped to a point, her merlot lips smiling seductively. I am unable to resist.

We hurry down the steps, my coat, which she is still wearing, nipping at her heels. In the tunnel, all is dark again. I spin her around and kiss her. I press her against the cold brick wall. I hike up her skirt, push aside her panties.

Birds-eye view: two shadows in the dark, covered by my overcoat. Strategically placed lines depict grinding motions. Unboxed, muffled grunts and moans in barely visible quotations, appear on either side of us.

"Not here," she whispers in my ear, pushing me gently away. "I prefer the comfort of my own bed." Her eyes glance sideways, towards the tunnel exit. I do not see what she is looking at, but I can guess.

He waits for us as we emerge onto the street. He steps into the white of a security light that shines above the tunnel's exit. The gun in his gloved hand appears to glint in the light, an illusion, a trick of the pen.

Instinctively, I reach into a pocket that is not there. It is then I realize she still has my knife. I feel it at the small of my back, point poking through my sweater, pricking my flesh. "Someone will see you, there will be witnesses," I say, grasping for some way out.

Full-page close-up: his face which is my face, only more gaunt and pale. He is my twin brother, having caught up with me at last. I don't care.

"You took her from me," he says.

Small frames overlap his face, in full color—a stark contrast to the shades of black I now inhabit, both of us as teenagers, twin brothers, thick and thin. Us sledding down a hill, joy on our faces. In the background lies our childhood home, slate roof, smoke drifting from the chimney. He and Alice watching TV as they sit on the floor of our house's rec-room, their faces aglow. They are holding hands. Alice is pretty, with gold curls and a dimple on her cheek. Me sitting nearby, watching them out of the corner of my eye, my face longing, filled with jealousy.

Me pretending to be him, taking Alice out in his car, her not noticing because we look so much alike.

Us out on the frozen lake to drive donuts and make out in the darkness.

Her realizing my deception, trying to get out of the car while it is moving on the ice. Me reaching out, trying to stop her, trying to explain.

The car splashing into a hole in the ice, me scrambling out, my expression one of exaggerated fear, mouth wide in a soundless scream. Alice trapped, pounding on the windshield as the car sinks rapidly in the frozen water.

Alice's funeral. A mahogany casket and aisles of mourners. My brother in tears, saying it is my fault, swearing revenge.

A return to darkness. A return to now. "I couldn't save her," I say. "There wasn't time."

"You should have died trying," he says.

A close-up of the gun. Click. Off goes the safety.

The three of us are all in the frame. My twin brother aims the gun at me. The woman I just met has my knife in my back. I stand between them, my hands spread in surrender. I only have one chance.

The action unfolds, frame by frame, in slow motion. I reach behind me, grab the girl's hand that holds the knife, twist it from her grip. It falls to the ground.

My brother raises the gun to eye level, fires. At the same moment, I crouch for the knife. The bullet hangs in mid-air, curved lines depicting its spiral. It goes through the woman's chest.

I pick up the knife and swing my arm around in one fluid motion. I slash my brother's wrist as he fires a second time. The gun falls to the ground, goes off again. Above us, a windowpane shatters. I bring the knife up and under his ribcage, but at the last moment, I cannot drive it in. I graze his belly.

Reflexively, he grabs his stomach, falls to his knees. In full frame, I loom over him, the only color the red mark across his abdomen, the bleeding knife in my hand.

He looks up at me, his eyes, my eyes, full of pain. "Kill me," he says. "Put me out of my misery."

If I let him live, I know he will come for me again. Yet he is and always will be my brother.

Behind me, the woman gasps for breath. The color is gone from her lips. I pull my overcoat from her shoulders and leave her shivering. Sirens wail in the distance. Above me, where the windowpane shattered, I hear a woman screaming. I cannot see it, but I know, the way things are known in stories, that the second wayward bullet must have hit the woman's child.

I put my overcoat back on, tuck my knife into the pocket. As I disappear into the darkness, my coat cocoons around me, guarding me against the wind.

Resurrectionists

Jacob and Isaac drove their spades deep, tossing shovelfuls of dirt high over their shoulders. Soil and sweat had embedded themselves into the hairs of their arms and chests. Their faces were as black as the minstrels they'd seen in vaudeville shows. They did not feel the chilled night air.

The cemetery rarely took time to bury the dead at a proper six feet anymore. After digging less than three feet down, the rich soil gave way to clay, and their spades struck the lid of a pine casket. Using their spades as levers, they hoisted the casket from its grave.

They pried off the lid, tilted the casket, and dumped the body back into the open hole. A teenage boy, crumpled and twisted, lay at the bottom of the grave. The funeral had been just that afternoon. A tombstone hadn't even been placed yet. The two men learned early on to dig up only the freshest bodies. The soil was less packed than those even a few months old, and there was less chance the casket would be rotted or infested with termites or carpenter ants.

Jacob gazed down at the teenager's body, making the sign of the cross.

"I don't know why you go in for all that mumbo-jumbo," Isaac said.

"Nothing wrong with having a little respect," Jacob replied, his voice muffled through his gauze mask.

They refilled the hole, pushing dirt onto the body with the backs of their spades. They picked up the empty casket and carried it down the gently sloping hill, past graves as old as the town. Their feet crunched fallen leaves as they followed the wrought iron fence that ran along the cemetery's edge. The moon, crooked sideways, shimmered between the boughs of trees, gnarled like old women's hands. Isaac walked in front. Jacob slowed his pace so as not to push Isaac too fast as he limped along.

Their cart waited near the cemetery's back gate. Old Galen stomped his hooves as Isaac and Jacob stacked the casket in back along with the four others they had already taken that night. "One more and we'll be set. Six caskets at five bucks a piece. Thirty bucks ain't bad." Isaac limped to the front of the cart, pulled out a bottle of rye. He drank three long swallows and passed the bottle to Jacob. Jacob pulled his mask down over his chin, wiped the lip of the bottle clean and took a sip.

"Wearing that thing won't help," Isaac said. "See people all over town with them on. They still get sick."

Jacob shrugged. "Figure it doesn't hurt."

The Spanish Influenza had spread quickly with the soldiers returning from Europe. It descended on the town of Four Banks, Ohio in late August. The town panicked as one person after another got sick and died. Mayor Westmoreland and the town council took emergency measures. Town meetings were canceled, assembly of more than three people was banned, and houses where someone had fallen ill were quarantined. The town's four pubs were closed to all but take-home sales. One hundred and twelve townspeople died in eight weeks. Young, old, rich, poor—the flu didn't play favorites.

Jacob and Isaac passed the bottle back and forth a couple more times, wiping it clean each time to avoid spreading anything. Leaving it in the back of the wagon, they returned to the cemetery, spades slung over their shoulders. They stopped at the nearest fresh grave, practically stumbling over the small mound of dirt in the dark. They began digging. The night was quiet. The air smelled of must. The moon became muted as if veiled by clouds even though the night was clear. An old ash grew beside the grave. Dead branches that had fallen from its upper reaches lay strewn around its trunk.

The work went slowly. The earth was slightly frozen, and they had to drive their spades in with all their weight to break the ground.

"It's too early for the ground to freeze. We haven't even had a frost. Maybe we should try another one," Jacob said.

"There aren't anymore. It was a slow day," Isaac replied.

"But we've hardly gone a foot down."

"Quit complaining or I won't ask you along next time."

Jacob and Isaac had been friends since childhood. At fourteen, they both left school and got jobs at the mill, loading flour onto barges. When the U.S. entered the Great War, Isaac got drafted, but for some reason, Jacob was passed over. He stayed behind while his best friend went off to fight in France, eventually taking a bayonet in the thigh. They almost had to amputate, but the surgeons managed to save the leg. Isaac was luckier than many, but he didn't think so.

"I'm going to be a gimp the rest of my life," he had said to Jacob one day. They were both working at the mill again. Business was booming supplying the military.

"Lot of guys don't come back," Jacob replied.

"What do you know about it?" Isaac said. "You weren't there. I don't even know why we stay friends."

Jacob took Isaac's abuse in stride. It was his way of making up for the fact that he had stayed home. The war continued, and sometimes Jacob thought about volunteering. But fear always stood between him and the enlistment office.

"No one knows what war's like unless they've been there. The people here don't know. I didn't get nothing for my trouble, compared to what I gave up." That's when Isaac told Jacob his scheme. There were two funeral homes in town. With all the deaths, caskets were in short supply. Take the caskets from one funeral home after the burial, remove the bodies, then sell them to the other for a tidy sum. That was the plan.

"That's stealing," Jacob had said.

"The dead don't care," Isaac had responded.

Jacob had a good job at the mill, but he knew if he didn't go along with Isaac on this, Isaac would never trust him again. The war had made Isaac bitter and irritable, especially with anyone he cared about, but he was Jacob's best friend. Jacob hoped that by sticking it out, the Isaac he knew from before the war, always ready with a story and a beer, would eventually return.

They continued digging through the night, spades chipping the hard soil—two feet…three feet…four feet. Jacob was beginning to wonder whether there was a grave at all, but Isaac insisted they continue. After a while, Jacob went back to the cart for the bottle. They finished it, letting the rye burn their throats.

"I hear they're close to banning alcohol," Jacob said, tossing the bottle onto the ground.

"Won't ever happen."

"They say liquor is evil."

Isaac leaned against his spade, examining the night sky. They stood in the grave, their chests even with the ground. "There was a little town near the front lines. I met a woman in a tavern, pretty, said she'd do anything for American dollars in this sexy French accent. We found a little spot in an abandoned barn. Woke up with my wallet stolen and the clap to boot. Risk my life for those people, and she goes and does something like that. Ungrateful wench. *She* was evil."

Only their foreheads were visible above the hole when they finally uncovered the coffin. They cleared the dirt off, revealing a mahogany casket with tight, heavily varnished grain. A rose was carved into the lid, the thorns sharp to the touch. The sides were decorated with delicate trim.

"This one ought to fetch us twenty-five, thirty dollars easy," Isaac said as they hoisted it out of the grave.

The lid was hinged and creaked as they opened it. A young woman lay on a bed of creamy silk. Pale, flawless skin, blond hair draped around her shoulders. Her heavy lids hinting at large, round eyes. She wore a purple dress of crushed velvet, a gold chain with a diamond pendant around her neck. A porcelain doll in its case.

Jacob looked at the name on the gravestone, Rosie Harwell. "I know who this is," he said, "We went to school with her."

Isaac eyed the body. His gaze stopped on the pendant. "Yeah, I remember. Stand-offish. Never would give me the time of day."

"She was always nice to me," Jacob said. "I remember how she used to look at my palm, claim she could see my future. Told me I'd be something someday."

"She was wrong about that."

Jacob shrugged. "Haven't seen her in years. She went to live with her grandmother in the eighth grade after her parents died. Her grandmother was a midwife over in Eastings. Never knew Rosie came back."

"Doesn't matter now," Isaac replied. He reached down, snapped the clasp of the gold chain as he snatched the pendant from Rosie's neck. "Booty," he said, placing the pendant and chain in his trouser pocket.

"Our deal was we leave the bodies alone," Jacob said.

"You said that, not me." Isaac started to tip the casket over like he was dumping grain from a wheelbarrow back at the mill.

Jacob put his hands on the casket to stop him. "Be careful."

Isaac let go of the casket. The body remained inside. He straightened, rushed at Jacob, throwing his weight into him and shoving him into the grave. Jacob landed flat on his back.

"I say what goes here," he said.

Jacob climbed out of the grave. He was a head taller than Isaac and outweighed him by thirty pounds. He could pound him into the ground if he wanted, but he couldn't hurt his oldest friend.

"I just want to give her some dignity," Jacob said.

"I remember right, you were sweet on her."

"Like I said, she was nice to me." Jacob gazed at her face, tilted his head to one side. "She's so beautiful."

"That's sick. Besides, morticians could even make *you* look good. Come on, give me a hand."

Jacob didn't move.

Isaac snarled, "Fine, we'll put her in nice, but it's on my say-so, not yours."

They gently laid the body in the grave. Jacob folded her arms across her chest, his hand brushing against her firm, round breasts. His flesh tingled. He became erect. He glanced at Isaac, embarrassed. His friend did not seem to notice.

They scooped a few shovelfuls of dirt onto the body, just enough to cover one of her legs and part of her stomach, when old Galen began to neigh. The two men became concerned that someone would hear. Isaac went to investigate.

Jacob stopped working. Rosie was perfect. He recalled one day, when they were playing together before the school bell rang. He had tried to impress her with a spider he had found. He held it out in his open palm. It crawled slowly towards the tips of his fingers. When she barely glanced at it. He tossed it to the ground, stomped it with his shoe.

"Don't do that," she had said. She was still a girl, her silken hair in braids, her face without makeup. She bent over the spider. Its torso was crushed, its legs spread at awkward angles. She moved in so close her lips almost touched it. She blew on it. To Jacob's surprise, the spider stirred. It rose up on its legs and scurried away. Later, he asked her how she did it. She answered with a smile that made his heart leap into his throat.

Jacob hopped into the hole. In the distance, he could hear Isaac yelling at Galen to calm down. He pulled down his mask, leaned over Rosie's face. She smelled of lavender. He paused, savoring. He kissed her slowly, longingly. He moved his tongue between her lips and entered her mouth. It was dry but tasted sweet. He ran a hand across her face, surprisingly warm, leaving a smudge of dirt on her cheek.

The horse stopped neighing. Jacob scurried out of the grave, placed his mask back over his mouth. By the time Isaac reappeared, Jacob was working quickly to cover up Rosie's body. All of her was covered except for the V at her neckline, and the soft line of her chin. Jacob had kissed her on impulse. He wondered if the dead were still contagious. He let out a reflexive cough.

"I think you should put the pendant back," he said to Isaac. "It was a gift from her grandmother. She gave it to her on her thirteenth birthday. Her grandmother died of pneumonia a few months later. They were very close. It's all she had to remember her by."

"How'd you know that?"

Jacob thought a moment. He wasn't sure. "She must have told me once."

"She's just worm food. It doesn't mean anything to her anymore."

"It matters to God."

"God is bunk. No God worth worshipping would have created trenches ripe with dysentery. No God would invent flamethrowers that burn you alive or mustard gas that sucks the breath from you or machine guns that mow you down by the dozen. No God, no sin, no retribution in the afterlife. We might as well take what we can while we're here."

They continued working. The first gray light of morning appeared just as they finished filling the grave. They lifted the ornate casket, carried it back to their cart. It was heavier than the others. The muscles in Jacob's arms and legs ached. He walked half asleep, his eyes nearly closed. Their shift at the mill started in a couple of hours.

Breath steamed from Galen's nostrils as they loaded the coffin into the wagon. Jacob suddenly found it hard to stand. He braced himself against his spade to keep his legs from giving out beneath him.

"Don't tell me you're getting sick," Isaac said. "And if you are, you're walking home. I didn't make it through the war to have some bug do me in."

Jacob leaned against the side of the wagon. "You know where the word 'flu' came from? It's from the Spanish, 'influenza,' or 'to be under the influence. Back in the Middle Ages, they believed that having the flu meant you were under the influence of the devil."

"What, you an encyclopedia now?"

Jacob had no idea where this information came from. He must have read it, but he could not recall where. "Ever think, maybe we're the ones under the devil's influence, stealing from graves?"

Isaac dismissed him with a wave of his hand. "You got it bad. Never seen it come on so quick." He tossed his spade into the back of the wagon, starting towards the front. "No way you're riding with me now."

"There's no cure. In ancient times, basil leaves mixed with dried ginger powder, milk, and sugar would be taken three to four times a day to try and cure it." Jacob paused. His head pounded. He felt chilled to his bones. "It didn't work, not for me, anyway."

"You're delirious," Isaac said. He started to climb into the wagon.

Jacob came up behind Isaac, raised his spade, brought it down on Isaac's head. Isaac fell face down in a bed of leaves. Blood dripped from the back of his scalp.

Old Galen snorted. Jacob unhitched him, smacked him on the hind. The horse started to make his way home. Jacob bent over Isaac, rummaging through his pockets until he found the pendant on its chain. The clasp broken, he tied the chain in a knot behind his neck. The diamond pressed against his skin, leaving a deep depression in his chest.

Jacob left the coffin-laden wagon and began to walk towards town, away from the cemetery. Skin slick with sweat, he suddenly realized how cold he was. Yanking off his mask, he inhaled the cool air deep.

How good it was to breathe again.

One Block at a Time

Ray stood in the department store toy aisle, browsing the sets of Wunderblocks as if he were picking out a thousand-dollar bottle of wine. The interlocking plastic blocks came in sets of varying size and complexity, complete with instructions for building spaceships and submarines, robots and dinosaurs. He had no interest in these—too fantastic. Some sets were media tie-ins with the latest *Terminator* and *Star Trek* sequels. Ray twisted his face with disgust at how marketing had cheapened his favorite childhood toy. Other sets were designed to build nothing in particular: packs of assorted blocks in all colors and sizes. He had most of these. No, what he was interested in was a set designed to make something real, something in the here and now. A set for building a fire station, a hospital, a house with flower boxes in its windows and a white picket fence; pieces for creating ambulances and tractors and pickup trucks with fat rubber tires and plastic, tinted windshields.

He picked up several boxes, studied them, shook them, listened to the pieces rattle. Finally, he settled on a set designed to build a gas station, complete with a garage for making repairs and a tow truck. He paid for it at the register with one-dollar bills and tips from bagging groceries at the West Side Co-op.

"Your son will love this," the cashier said. She was an older woman, obviously forced to work into retirement, with curly white hair and an orange smock. In response, Ray nodded and smiled. To think he had a son young enough to play with blocks, to think he was buying the set for anyone other than himself.

Ray took the 394 bus back to his one-bedroom garden apartment. Sheets hung over the windows for curtains. An air mattress, which served as both his couch and bed lay in the living room, along with a small TV and a tall stack of books he had packed away when Terese kicked him out. The cramped kitchen had no room for a table; he ate at the kitchen counter on a wooden stool. He had a coffee maker and a toaster on the counter, and nothing but peanut butter and jelly in the pantry and some leftover frozen pizza in the fridge.

Kneeling in his living room, Ray opened the set of blocks he had just bought and spread them over the worn carpet. He leafed through the instructions for building the gas station, tossed them aside. He didn't need someone else telling him what to do. The set came with some specialty pieces, including the chassis of a motorcycle and two fuel pumps. He discarded these as well. He had no use for pieces that were only good for building a single item. He preferred the traditional shapes from his childhood—cubes and cylinders and slanted pieces used for roofing. Two plastic people, two inches tall, came with the set: a mechanic with overalls painted on his body and a cap to cover his bald head, and a woman with wavy dark hair and glasses. He kept these, even though they were pre-made. As hard as he tried to build people from scratch using the tiniest blocks available, he could never get their faces right. The premade ones always had faces that were bright and open, always smiling.

Ray built a gas station, only his was different from the one pictured on the box. The columns that held the roof above the fuel pumps were not straight but stepped and angled. The station was supposed to be yellow with a red foundation, red doors, red windows. He mixed and matched the colors, built a red flower into one wall as if it were graffiti. He left another wall open. It was summer, he decided, and the building would be too stuffy otherwise. The crank that lifted the cars for servicing was clumsy, he oiled it so it ran smooth. He improved on the tow truck as well. He increased the cab size, lengthening the towing device so it could haul a larger vehicle more easily.

When he was finished, at about two in the morning, he carefully lifted the gas station and carried it into the bedroom. The floor of the ten-by-ten room was covered with miniature block buildings. There were tiny houses with yellow roofs and open windows, a police station, a fire station, a town hall with a clock tower. There were two- and three-story buildings with big picture windows along a main street lined with wide sidewalks, restaurants and shops, and even a small art gallery. Plastic trees expertly trimmed and flowers always in bloom dotted the landscape. The town was laid out in a grid pattern, with wide boulevards and well-kept lanes and a minimum of traffic—cars and trucks that never blew through stop signs and always obeying the speed limit.

Ray set the gas station down between Main Street and a parkway of single-family homes. He straightened and, like a proud new proprietor opening his doors on the first day of business, crossed his arms and waited for cars, tanks empty, to arrive for their fill-ups and perhaps even an oil change.

"I'M WORRIED ABOUT YOU, DAD." Brie stood in the threshold of the bedroom, looming over Ray as he sat cross-legged on the floor, arranging the people in the park he had created for his little town, complete with benches and a pathway and a bandshell for concerts on Saturday nights.

Ray did not look up at his daughter. "Your mother doesn't care about me anymore," he said.

Brie leaned against the doorjamb. She was tall and lithe. She had wanted to be a dancer when she was a younger, but after years of rejection, she took a managing job for a catering company. "Just because she couldn't live with you anymore doesn't mean Mom doesn't care. She puts on a good front, like always, but this has hurt her, too."

Ray turned to his daughter. "Tell me, do I seem happier now than I was then?"

Brie twirled her long blond hair with her fingers, something she did when she was reluctant to tell the truth. Ray recalled how he used to run his hand through it when she was a child, to lull her to sleep. "You're not brooding like you used to. But this—this is a bit crazy."

"When I was a boy, Wunderblocks were only sold in Europe, through catalogs and a few import shops. Used to get a new set every birthday and Christmas. Never the big sets though—the galleons and starships—too expensive. Now, you can buy them in any discount store. Never thought I'd own so many."

"I think you ought to see someone."

"Tell your mother I'm fine, just fine."

"She has nothing to do with this."

"She told you to come. We were married twenty-two years. I know that much." He set a girl with pigtails on one of the benches he had just created. He had trouble securing her in place, pushed a little too hard, and the bench collapsed. He picked up the pieces, started to rebuild the bench. "They aren't like real life. When they break, you can always put them back together again."

RAY MOVED DEFTLY AS THE GROCERIES of a young mother with an infant in tow rolled down the conveyor belt, bagging them as carefully as a mason lays bricks, stacking heavy items on the bottom, mixing frozen and chilled items to keep the chilled items cold, packing vegetables and fruit together, meats in a separate bag, the bread, eggs, and other fragile items on top. He filled the bags for maximum efficiency, never allowing them to overflow while still ensuring they could stand on their own.

Whether the young mother or any other customer at the West Side Co-op noticed his attention to his craft as he loaded their carts, he couldn't say. Only a few gave him a second glance. It didn't matter. He didn't do the job for them. He did it for himself and, of course, for Mariah.

"You know, you could make things easier on yourself if you used more bags, didn't pack them so carefully," Mariah said after the mother had gone. Her baby had started crying just as they were heading out the door. Mariah was half his age and looked much younger than that, with short, dark hair and a waif's body. Ray had a crush on her. Whenever he had a chance, he would strike up conversations with her: awkward, nothing conversations, about how slow it was, about whether payday was this Friday or next Friday. They'd share jokes, and complain in soft whispers about their boss, Clive, who changed schedules on a whim and acted as if breaks were optional, especially on a busy Saturday afternoon.

Mariah wore several bracelets on her right wrist, had a tattoo of a rose just below her collarbone. Her skin was pale, her face round. She had a lilting laugh that Ray seldom heard, and a crooked smile she hardly ever used, even on customers. Clive instructed them all to smile more at his morning huddles when he'd try to psych them all up with slogans he'd read from the myriad of business books he kept in his office.

When it was busy, they couldn't talk, but still Ray reveled in Mariah's voice: soft, yet with an edge. He would comfort himself with the task at hand: how to fit as much into a paper sack as possible without the handles breaking or the bread getting squished or the bananas bruising. All the while, he would listen to Mariah's voice and, in the back of his head, wonder how to build on the little town that was becoming a big town back in his apartment.

Ray and Mariah didn't usually get their lunch breaks at the same time, but this day was different. Ray's heart lifted a little as he thought about spending an entire half hour with her, but when her boyfriend, Kai, inevitably showed up, Ray resigned himself to sitting alone in the lunchroom while they went out back to share a cigarette.

The lunchroom was just off the storeroom, cinderblock walls and metal chairs around a couple of folding tables, vending machines, a microwave, the time clock and a bulletin board where the legally required posters about workers' compensation and minimum wage were covered over by notes from Clive to keep the room clean, and that being late could result in "disciplinary action." Ray was nibbling at a cheese sandwich and sipping a cream soda when Mariah returned. Usually, she was back late from her lunch when Kai came by and would receive admonishment from Clive. He'd do this in front of the rest of the staff, sometimes even in front of customers. This time, she returned early. Ray smiled at her. She looked at him, her eyes swollen and wet with tears, then turned away, and hurrying onto the sales floor.

Later, while Ray stocked the shelves in the canned soup aisle, he heard a loud voice coming from the registers. At first, he figured it was one of the many homeless men who lived in the neighborhood and wandered in to use the restroom without anyone noticing, maybe lift an apple from produce or—for one or two crazies—rant at the shoppers and the staff about the president being Hitler, or the FBI being a cult, or that rats could talk, or whatever their paranoid-schizophrenic fantasy happened to be. It was safest to ignore these people. But when Ray heard Mariah's name, he stuck his head from out of the aisle. Kai was behind Mariah's register. He held her wrist tight, and was shouting about a call she had made on her cell phone. Clive was standing several feet away, pretending to inspect a candy rack for outdated chocolate bars in aisle five. He wasn't brave unless you worked for him, and Mariah's boyfriend didn't work for him.

A middle-aged woman with close-cropped hair wheeled her cart up to Mariah's register. Kai let go of Mariah and stormed out of the store.

TERESE HAD BEEN LEAVING VOICEMAILS on Ray's phone for the past several days. He hadn't bothered to call her back. She'd kicked him out, and now he was supposed to call her? This time when she called, he was lying on his air mattress, reading a book on the architects of the 1893 Columbia Exposition and wondering how he could incorporate some of their Neoclassical domes and pillars into his modest village in the other room. He sighed and picked up the phone.

"Brie tells me you're playing with toys," she said.

"What of it?"

"It's not like you," she said.

"It's not like how you *wanted* me to be, you mean."

There was a long pause. "Look, Ray. I know you think I threw you out, but I didn't. You could have gotten help. I asked you a thousand times. But you didn't. I couldn't handle your moods anymore."

"I'm not in a mood now."

"No," she said. "You are. But this mood is different, this mood seems—"

"Content?"

There was another pause, as if she wanted to argue with him, but decided against it. "I just want to let you know I still care. Goodbye, Ray."

RAY'S MOTHER DIED OF EMPHYSEMA at the age of sixty-three. She used to sneak smokes into her hospital bed, light up while oxygen was pumped through a tube in her nose. Ray thought it a filthy habit, but smoking was an excuse to be with Mariah when Kai wasn't around, and she would go outside to have a cigarette.

"You don't smoke, do you?" Mariah asked.

"I'm just starting up again," Ray replied, suddenly conscious of how awkward he must look.

"Clive makes you want more than just cigarettes."

They were at the loading dock behind the store. The sweltering summer day had given way to a warm evening that was on the threshold of bearable. The scent of garbage from the dumpsters filled the air.

Kai came down the alley. He walked ramrod straight, but as he neared, Ray could smell the liquor on his breath, seeping from his pores. "Who's the old guy?" He pointed at Ray, his bony arms flexing beneath his black T-shirt. He wore jeans despite the heat, torn in several places and splashed with paint.

"He works here," Mariah said.

Kai stared at Ray, his eyes bloodshot. He had skin almost as pale as Mariah's and hair that was unnaturally dark, short, and spiked. A scruff of beard clung to his chin as if glued there. His thin lips seemed incapable of a smile. "Get lost. This is private."

Ray looked to Mariah. Mariah nodded. Sensing it was okay, he turned back into the store.

It was a busy afternoon. Ray was too lost in bagging for customers to realize that Mariah hadn't returned from her break. Twenty minutes later, Clive was asking everyone where she was. When he asked Ray, he told him they had been on break together but hadn't seen her since. Clive walked away, shaking his head, muttering something about canning her for blowing off work.

Ray closed with Clive and a couple of cashiers, one of whom Clive had asked to work late to help cover Mariah's abandoned shift. Ray said his goodnights and meandered home, the streets dark except for the dim light from second-story apartments, streetlamps like halos, and a few passing cars. A few young men swaggered by him from the other direction, the whites of their eyes bright as they stared him down, sized him up. Ray had been walking these streets at night for several weeks now. He knew the routine. He made eye contact. They left him alone. Still, a lump formed in his throat as he listened to their footsteps behind him. He jumped when he felt a tug on his sleeve.

Mariah stood behind him, her face shadowed by a streetlight. "I can't go home," she said.

Ray walked her back to his apartment, fumbled with the keys as he unlocked the door. He offered to make coffee, but she only wanted water. As she sat on the stool at the counter of his tiny kitchen, sipping water from a jelly jar, Ray examined her for some sign of bruising, but saw nothing. Still, he could tell by the way she held herself that she was hurting.

"Kai's a really talented artist, murals mostly," she said.

Ray did not reply. He understood enough to know that great art didn't make a great man. He also understood that wasn't what Mariah needed to hear right now. Right now, all she needed was someone to listen.

"I dropped out of school to be with him," she said. "We met when I was a sophomore. He was a senior about to graduate. He said if I loved him, I'd follow him here. Said he had an agent lined up. A gallery was interested in his work. That was a year ago. Hasn't done anything but drink the last six months. My parents were so pissed. They wanted me to go on to law school."

"What did you want?"

Mariah shrugged. "I guess I never thought about it. It's never been about me."

Ray knew from his own experience that she was lying. She had probably asked herself that question a thousand times.

It wasn't the question that scared her. It was the answer. "I always wanted to be an architect," Ray said. "The program in school was too grueling, though, and it paid dirt when you were all through. For the first years, anyhow. So, I ended up in sales. Made good money, too."

"And you left it to bag groceries?"

"Turns out, I don't like people all that much. I'm good with them, built a book of business on relationships and trust. Sold everything from medical equipment to networking software in my career. Still, I had to drag myself into every call. I cringed every time the phone rang or an email popped up. I needed a change. I read about this guy, lost his high-paying job and started working at a coffee shop. Happier now than he's ever been."

"And you?"

"It hasn't worked out that well. People buy groceries." Ray excused himself to use the bathroom. He came out to find Mariah in the bedroom. He had recently added a streetcar to Main Street, and she was on her hands and knees looking inside the little car at the commuters and the ticket agent, all smiling and happy to be on their way.

Ray braced himself for a response much like Brie's. He braced himself for the end of a friendship.

"Amazing!" was all she said.

In his head, Ray knew he could have her then. She was vulnerable, and his eccentricity impressed her. She went for artists after all, and what was this, but art? He took her by the hand and helped her up, leading her out of the room. They sat on his inflatable mattress, hand-in-hand. He turned off the overhead lights so that a tiny lamp in the corner was the only light. He turned on the radio. The station played acoustic versions of rock hits and, while he couldn't place the tune, it seemed appropriate. Mariah lay back on the bed. Ray settled next to her. She folded her hands across her stomach, her eyes wide, her face blank. Ray ran his fingers through her hair. She closed her eyes, made a soft purring sound. "My dad used to do that."

Ray stopped. He picked himself up on one elbow, looked down at Mariah, that soft, young, fleshy face, the face of a child. He remained next to her, not touching her, as she drifted off to sleep. Then he made a bed at her feet with one of the pillows and an extra blanket and hoped the snoring his wife used to complain about wouldn't wake her.

THE DAY MARIAH CAME TO WORK in long sleeves even though it was ninety degrees outside, Ray knew something would have to be done about Kai.

"What is it? Burns, bruises?"

Mariah didn't reply. The din of nearby street traffic cut through the silence. They were in the alley, sharing another break. Mariah had kept her job only by promising to work extra shifts. It didn't hurt that they were shorthanded because Clive had trouble keeping cashiers for more than a month or two before they quit out of disgust.

Ray had given up the pretense of smoking. Instead, he watched the way Mariah's mouth wrapped around the cigarette, how smoke wafted from her parted lips. "You should never have gone back to him. Leave him now. Come stay with me until you get things figured out."

Mariah shook her head. "He said he was sorry. He's sold a painting. Not for much. He's taking me to dinner tonight."

"He doesn't smile," Ray said. "Even unhappy people smile now and then. Even you."

She grinned at that.

Later that evening, Ray sat as a god amidst his tiny town, setting up a road crew to build a pedestrian bridge over Main Street, which was becoming increasingly busy with cars, motorcycles, and delivery vans. It was then the idea struck him. Mariah's good fortune with Kai wouldn't last. When things did come to a head with Kai, Ray intended to be ready.

Ray dumped a box of blocks of various shapes and sizes and colors onto the floor, sorted through them to find the ones he needed. He worked quickly, without thought to color or form, only function. Once it was complete, he examined what he had made, hefted it in his hand and nodded, fully satisfied.

IT WAS DINNERTIME. The lull between commuters picking up groceries on their way home and night owls doing their late shopping. Clive had the day off, so no one was working all that hard. Mariah was the only cashier open, but without customers around she was reading one of the celebrity gossip magazines stocked near the counter. Ray filled the downtime by ensuring all the bag holders were fully stocked. The bulge in the pocket of his smock pushed against his stomach. He had been carrying it around for the past three days but still hadn't gotten used to it.

Kai strode in, approached Mariah. He spoke quietly for a change. Ray was at the far end of the line of registers, so he couldn't make out what he was saying. Mariah was shaking her head to whatever it was. Kai took a bill from his pocket, handed it to her. She opened her drawer, apparently to make change. He pushed her out of the way, reached into her till, emptied the twenties slot. She called after him, but he was already halfway out the door. She turned to Ray, her eyes welling with tears. Clive would certainly fire her for this. He would blame her no matter what she or Ray said.

Ray ran after Kai, who appeared not to be in any hurry; it wasn't hard to catch up to him. Ray wasn't used to running, though, and was breathing hard when he tapped Kai on the shoulder. "The money," Ray panted. "Give it back."

From his smock, Ray pulled what he had made a few nights before. He placed it against Kai's back. Kai turned.

He was staring at a pistol made of Wunderblocks, the mismatch of colors making it appear like some sort of dream gun. Its barrel was short and obscenely thick—a toy, nothing more. "Give it back," Ray said.

Ray expected Kai to laugh, or at least grin, upon seeing the gun. Instead, he just grunted, started walking again. Ray fired. It had a surprisingly powerful kick. Dozens of tiny blocks flew from its muzzle, scattering like a broken rainbow.

RAY CAME OUT OF THE BATHROOM, dressed and showered. Mariah sat at the counter, a history textbook open in front of her. She had just started taking classes again at the local community college. "You look nice," she said. "I can see why Terese wants you back."

"We're taking it slow," Ray reminded her. He and his ex-wife had been talking on the phone regularly, and had finally decided that a "date" was in order. He was taking her to dinner, a local, good but cheap Thai place that Mariah had introduced him to. His new job hadn't started paying yet.

Mariah hopped off the stool, went to Ray, straightened his collar. "When do you start on your first project?"

"The blocks should be here tomorrow."

Mariah had read about a man in Tennessee who made all kinds of things out of Wunderblocks on commission. He ordered blocks by the tens of thousands over the internet. He created statues for children's museums, toy store displays, ten-foot-tall buildings, life-sized animals, full-size gazebos. He'd even made a desk for an eccentric IT executive in Silicon Valley that was ergonomically correct. Turned out, the Tennessee man was swamped and couldn't keep up with his workload. Ray wasn't the only one who recalled Wunderblocks from his childhood so fondly. At Mariah's urging, Ray sent the man photos of his creations, and he offered to send some work Ray's way. The first project was a replica of an office building in Cincinnati that had just been built, to be placed in its foyer.

Ray wrung his hand.

"Still hurts, huh?" Mariah asked.

"Not too bad," Ray replied. When he fired his homemade gun, it shattered. Tiny pieces of plastic embedded themselves into his right hand, colorful freckles.

Ray went into the bedroom. He had nearly finished dismantling the village. He would need the space for paying projects, after all. Still, he kept Main Street and the park that adjoined it. It would be easy to move if it got in the way.

He left the people in place as well. A child and his mother watching the ducks that swam in the pond, a couple walking down the path, a deliveryman on a bicycle taking a shortcut, and most recently, a man standing just outside the park, on the street corner, as if waiting for a bus that would never arrive. Ray had made this one himself, finally able to get the face right. A tuft of hair dotted his chin, and unlike the rest of the people, he was not smiling; his face fixed in a permanent frown.

Beneath the Linden Tree

What sounded like burners firing from a hot air balloon roared overhead. Melia ran out into the yard, hoping to see it up close. She loved the balloons. On pleasant summer days like this one, they gave rides over the river valley to tourists. The balloons hardly ever came in this far, and when they did, they soared high. Mere dots against the sky. This one, however, sounded low to the ground. She imagined it a kaleidoscope of color, its basket skimming the trees, almost within reach. She needed some joy, even if it was fleeting.

Melia looked up but didn't see a balloon, just a few high, feathery clouds. Dejected, she started back inside, then something caught her eye. A tail, spiked with purple scales, iridescent in the sun. It made a wide, sweeping motion, then disappeared behind Omi's garage.

Ever since the funeral, Melia had avoided Omi's house. It sat just across the alley from her own, detached garages facing one another, Melia's a deep crimson, Omi's a periwinkle blue.

Curious, Melia hurried across her backyard, overgrown, lawn all creeping Charlie and crabgrass, some boxwoods yellow from too little water, too much sun. All of it dominated by an ancient, dying elm, leaves providing too little shade.

Heading out her back gate, faded wooden pickets always sticking, Melia didn't notice she was bare foot until she was in the alley, the blacktop hot against her soles. She ignored the pain. More times than she could count, Omi had admonished her for going without shoes. "Those are more paws than feet," she'd say with a scowl that was more smile than frown.

At Omi's own wrought iron gate, freshly painted like new, Melia paused. She hadn't been in Omi's garden since the old woman passed away. She couldn't bring herself to go to the services or to the luncheon held there afterward. Instead, she stayed in her room, keeping her earbuds in, music turned up loud so she couldn't hear the laughter of those paying their last respects wafting across the alley. How could they laugh when Omi was gone?

The gate had a lock. "To keep rabbits out," Omi would joke, admitting she didn't even know where the key was and wouldn't lock it regardless. With a trembling hand, Melia unhooked the latch, eased the gate open just enough to slide through. As she stepped across the stones that cut a path between the garage and a neatly pruned hedgerow, she half expected to turn the corner and see Omi's well-kept garden in shambles, with overgrown shrubs, and withering roses, and flower beds overwhelmed with weeds.

It wasn't though. Except for a thistle or dandelion sprouting up here or there, which Omi never would have allowed, the garden looked almost as well tended as the last time Melia saw it. It was the same day Omi had complained how tired she was and how she needed a nap. Melia felt guilty for not realizing what this meant. Omi never took naps. She would never see her friend again, had no chance to say goodbye.

The garden was Omi's pride and joy. A tiny, manicured lawn surrounded by all manner and color of irises and petunias and lilies. Ivy grew thick. Grape vines climbed up trellises. White and pink roses bloomed. "Never red," Omi had told her once. "I'm too old for love." In one corner stood a dwarf maple that in fall turned a flaming red. A linden grew tall and straight just off center from the middle of the lawn, providing just the right amount of shade for the little brick patio, with its café table and two chairs, where Omi and Melia would sit and drink lemonade "With a little extra something for me," Omi would say with a wink after a morning of weeding and watering and pruning.

Someone sat at the café table now. An old man with skin that looked like he had spent ages in the sun. He wore a loose shirt and loose pants, sandals, and a floppy, wide brimmed hat. He wore dark sunglasses, but the movement of his head told her he was scanning the garden as if looking for something, finally settling on Melia's tiny frame, her rolled up cut-offs betraying bruised and cut knees, her tank top showing off shoulders specked with scars from scratched mosquito bites.

Melia scowled, as if to let him know that this was not his place. This was Omi's, and to some extent hers. More than once, Omi told her she should play with friends her own age. Melia would respond that she'd rather spend time with her. Omi would turn away, but not before Melia glimpsed that grin of hers, amused and knowing with a hint of mischief.

The man scowled back at her. Melia wondered if she was being mocked, then concluded she was. She turned to leave. There was no tail, no sign of the creature it had belonged to, not even a footprint in the grass to show it had ever been. A trick of the light, or what her teacher noted on her last report card as an overactive imagination. Besides, it hurt just to be there. Without Omi, it felt so empty and colorless, no matter how vibrant the flowers may be.

"You must be Melia," the man said. His voice came from the back of his throat, like a wolf's growl.

The hairs on Melia's nape, cut short for summer, stood up on end. The sound of his voice and the fact he knew her name, sent her running. She hadn't been scared at first, but now, all those horror stories they told her in school about being wary of strangers flooded her mind. She hurried to the back gate, but found it locked. She heard the man coming up behind her, his footsteps surprisingly heavy. She started to scramble up the gate. A hand clamped her shoulder, more gently than she would have imagined. The man guided her back down to the ground.

"Please, don't go. I was her friend, too."

Melia turned towards him. She pressed her back against the gate as if its bars, on the wrong side, would offer her some protection. Her lower lip trembled. She thought she was going to wet herself.

The man sensed her fear, backed away, arms wide, palms open. He smiled, teeth white, except for one his upper canine which shone a hint of gold. Melia might have made ready friends with Omi, but she had a pleasant smile. This man had a sharper grin. It was that smile of Omi's that drew her to the old woman in the first place, that and the lilt in her voice.

"You there," Omi called from her yard into the alley one day. Melia was bouncing a ball against the garage door, counting how many times she could catch it without it hitting the ground. It was only June, but already looked to be a long, lonely summer. No kids in the neighborhood, and her parents weren't the playing type. "I could use your help."

Melia hesitated.

"Well, come on, are you a good neighbor or not?" Omi said. She was a small woman with a round face on a petite body. There was nothing remarkable about her, except for the fact that she had the bluest eyes Melia had ever seen, strangely specked with purple, so that Melia thought they must be contacts.

In the garden, Omi pointed to a bucket of tulip bulbs. "Hand me those," she said. Melia did as she was told, while Omi stooped over a sunny spot in the yard, buried them in the soil. When she was finished, Omi wiped her brow with a gloved hand, mud smearing across her forehead. "Come back tomorrow. We have roses to prune."

The next day, Melia returned, and showed up almost every day since. It wasn't until she had worked with Omi for a while that she realized the old lady didn't need any help from a young girl to keep her garden. That it wasn't she who was helping Omi, but the other way around.

"How did you know Omi?" Melia asked now, thinking if they were talking, the man wouldn't hurt her.

He laughed a rough laugh. "Omi, I like that. I'm sure she did, too. Your Omi, Renate, and I grew up together. Played together in the open sky."

Melia thought this a strange thing to say but didn't mention it. Sometimes, old people said odd things.

The man's hands dropped to his sides. Melia's body tightened. Her eyes darted from place to place, seeking some escape. The man held up his hands again, higher this time, as if in surrender. "I understand, we get a bad reputation. Me, and those like me."

With a slow, careful movement, so as not to startle her again, he lowered his hands, removed his sunglasses, folded them into the breast pocket of his shirt. His eyes were yellow, speckled green. Enough like Omi's for her to drop her guard, but only slightly.

"Oh, they're real," the man said, as if reading her thoughts. "We can take many shapes, but the eyes never change."

It dawned on Melia then. "The tail?"

The man, who she now realized was not a man, nodded. "Sometimes it's hard to be subtle."

"And Omi?"

He nodded again. "She left something. Beneath the linden tree. Do you know where she keeps the shovels?"

Melia gestured to the garage. He disappeared through the back door. It was her chance to run, but she stayed where she was. He returned with a pair of spades, their blades black from heavy use. He handed one to her. She took it.

The two walked out to the linden tree, Melia careful to keep him in front of her. As he set his shovel into the soil

Melia let out a tiny yelp. "Omi would be upset, us digging here. We could damage the roots."

He put his foot on the spade, but did not push it in. "You care about this garden almost as much as she did."

"I care about Omi more. Someone else will buy this place. They might tear it all out to make room for a pool. Worse, they might just leave it to rot. Too busy, like my parents," Melia said.

"Not much for gardening, huh?"

"Have you seen our yard? They aren't much for anything but work," *They aren't even about me*, she wanted to add.

"Well, we aren't here to destroy this wonderful garden," he said. "We're here to save it. Renate knew she wouldn't be around forever, so she asked me for this favor." He drove the spade into the ground and motioned Melia to do the same. Together, they soon had a hole about two feet deep and two feet around. "I think you'll have to do the rest by hand," he said.

Melia knelt in the soft, black soil and reached into the hole, amazed that their blades never hit even the tiniest of roots. She began to dig with her hand, pulling up tiny handfuls of dirt. She felt something squirm in her fingers. An earthworm. The first time she had encountered one, she screamed, but Omi just smiled that smile of hers and said they helped the garden grow. This one didn't bother her at all.

After a few handfuls, her hand hit something. "I think it's a rock," she said.

He knelt beside her. Together they cleared the dirt away from the object. Working as one, like she used to do with Omi, Melia found that her fear had disappeared.

They lifted the object from the hole. It was not like any rock Melia had ever seen. It was perfectly smooth, ovoid, and glistened a deep green in the sun.

"An egg?"

"Sort of," he replied. "It was Renate's, but you can't crack it. There's no yolk, no white, nothing will hatch from it."

He let it go. Melia held it in both her hands, surprised at how light it was.

"Now, it's yours," he said.

Melia tilted her head and squinted at him.

"Your Omi, she was yours, wasn't she? She could never have children, so she had this garden. Like you said, once the house is sold, the garden will most likely go to rot. Omi couldn't have that, and she couldn't have you lose it, along with losing her. She wanted you to have this. In her own small way, she wanted to give you *both*."

"What do I do with it?"

He nodded toward her own house. "You have your own garden to tend." He put a hand on Melia's shoulder, then turned away. She looked down at the stone, the rock, the egg, whatever you might call it. When she looked up again, he was gone.

Melia heard the same rush she had heard before. She gazed to the sky just in time to see the long purple body, flecked blue, snake up high into the air. It flew without wings, like a snake moving through the grass. Melia continued watching until he became lost in the wisp of a distant cloud.

Burying the stone in her own yard, beneath the dying elm, Melia sat in the grass and looked around her, tired and sweaty, her mind already filled with ideas of what could be planted where and of how she could steal cuttings and bulbs from Omi's garden when no one was around. Tomorrow, the hard work of weeding and cleanup would begin.

Melia laid back on the ground. She looked up through the leaves of the tree. Perhaps it was the way the sun hit them, or that imagination of hers again, or something else, but they seemed just a shade greener, just a bit more alive, than before.

My Heart Is Yours to Break

I pack my heart in a shoebox, wrap it in bubble wrap. I seal it with thick packaging tape and label it with a fat black marker. I do not include a return address. You would know who it was from.

The postal clerk asks if the box is fragile. I hesitate a moment, lie, and tell her no. When she asks if the box contains any perishable or hazardous items, I lie and tell her no again. As she sticks postage on the package and lifts it off the counter, I wonder how good her hearing is, how sensitive her touch. Will she hear the telltale *thu-thump, thu-thump, thu-thump* beneath the lid? She tosses the package in a bin piled high with cardboard boxes, tubes, and oversized envelopes, takes my cash, and calls for the next customer in line.

YOU FIND THE BOX WAITING for you after work, set outside your apartment door. You place it on the kitchen table, slit it open with a paring knife. Pulling off the lid, you look down at my heart, nestled in the bubble wrap. You shove the lid back on the box and slump into a nearby chair.

The other night at dinner, you were bored with our conversation. You twirled your pasta with your fork without eating it, alternated your gaze between the red and white checks in the tablecloth and the servers passing by. I told you what I was capable of, a vain attempt to impress you. "Extractions are a simple matter of knowing the proper incantation and having a sharp scalpel," I said. You perked up when I told you this, your eyes, gray as a summer storm, suddenly intent. You did not believe me, but you found me instantly fascinating all the same.

"So why aren't you a surgeon?" you asked skeptically.

"Too many rules about what you can and can't do," I explained. "I want freedom to experiment."

You took me to your bed that night—lavender skin, rose-bud lips, slender hands, the sweet taste of Riesling on your breath. You even let me spend the night, made me think you cared. All so you could tell your friends you slept with a madman. Complete with wide-eyed stares and long, tangled hair. So far removed from the men you usually date. Handsome but dull men with tailored suits and luxury sedans; dry conversations and sex by the numbers.

I know you weren't lying when you told me I was the best you had in a long while. I was not merely bragging when I told you I was full of surprises.

You pour yourself a white Russian, your favorite. You down it before finding the nerve to open the box again. You are fascinated by how small my heart is, barely the size of your fist. You inspect the places where it has been severed from the aorta and pulmonary artery, the superior and inferior vena cava. Clean and delicate cuts made with surgical precision. You are amazed that it still beats; slow but steady.

Is this some sort of suicide note, meant to torture you, to show you what you've driven me to? Van Gogh's ear taken to the extreme?

You shouldn't have led me on, slept with me, used me as a diversion, a lark. Maybe you should have spoken to me in person. Maybe you shouldn't have answered my repeated calls with a text, saying I was not your type, that you needed a man more grounded in reality. I could not give you what you needed.

You notice me finally, standing across the street, watching. My hands deep in my pockets, my neck craned towards your third-floor window. Our eyes meet. I take out a cigarette, light it, my moves sloth-like and deliberate.

You gulp down a second drink. It slowly dawns on you that my heart is a gift. The one thing I could give you that no other man could—or wouldn't even if he knew the words to say—even if he had my skill with a knife.

A part of you does not want this gift, this responsibility. You want to wrap it back up, return to sender. Or maybe just toss it in the alley dumpster. Rat food, nothing more.

You pop the bubble wrap between your fingers to the rhythm of my heart—*pu-pop, pu-pop, pu-pop*. Your ego surges with the thought that some man would put so much trust in you, could love you so. Even if that man was me.

My heart feels like so much raw meat as you lift it from the box. Blood seeps through your fingers. Your hands shake. You hold my life in your palms. How easy it would be to tighten your grip, make the beating stop.

But you are not a cruel person. You never meant to hurt me. You are human, nothing more. You set my heart back in the box, place the bubble wrap around it, like tucking a child into bed.

Reaching beneath my shirt, I scratch at the scar along the lower left side of my chest.

I have no breath.

My body is oddly silent.

Medusa Night

I sleep, curled into a ball, covers over my head. My mother taps me on the shoulder, tells me it's time to wake up. It is not my mother's voice. Her tone is uncharacteristically gentle. She has never woken me for school before. Usually, I'm the one who gets her out of bed. Yet, I know, somehow, it's her.

My eyes blink open. It is still night. A streetlamp shines through a crack in my curtain. My mother looms. She wears her tattered terry cloth bathrobe, the missing sash revealing the rolls of her stomach. Her overbearing rose perfume fills the air. But her face is sallow, her skin a sickly gray. Her hair is full of snakes, intertwined and writhing. My mother smiles, thin and lipless. I throw the covers over my head. She says my name. The snakes hiss.

A lump forms in my throat. My heart races. A sliver of light shines through a gap between my blanket and sheet. I move quickly to close it. She says my name again. I do not move. I hold my breath. The hissing stops. I hear footsteps, heading away, then silence. I dare to let out a gasp of air. A dream, a nightmare. We are learning Greek mythology in school. Perseus and Athena's shield, the Gorgon in her cave. That's all this is. Still, I cannot move.

It's hot beneath my blanket. I wipe cold sweat from my brow. I try to go back to sleep, but each time I close my eyes,

I see my mother's smile. I see the snakes, intertwined, nipping at one another with small but sharp teeth.

I whimper like a baby. I hope that my mother will hear me, come to me, comfort me in a way she hasn't done in a long while. Not the creature of my nightmare. The mother of my dreams.

She does not come.

When I was little, she would sit at my bedside and read to me each night. *Curious George* and *Green Eggs and Ham* and *Where the Wild Things Are*. Afterwards, she would cuddle up next to me, kiss me on the cheek, tell me she loved me. In those days, I believed her.

I let out another whimper, louder this time. From her own room across the hall, my mother calls my name, her voice sleepy and slurred. The voice I've grown accustomed to. A voice that is no dream.

Inch by inch, I pull my covers back. The streetlamp still casts soft shadows on the far wall. My alarm clock shows 3:34 a.m. in bright square numbers. I am alone. I will myself to get up.

My mother's door is ajar. She sits up on one elbow, her hair cut short, the same as it's always been. She asks me what is wrong. In a childlike voice, I tell her I had a bad dream and can't sleep.

Neither can I, she tells me. She draws back the sheet absentmindedly draped over her. I enter her room, kicking an empty bottle as I draw near. Her rose perfume can't cover the stench of her breath, the odor emanating through her pores. Still, I crawl in beside her. She covers me with the sheet. I am suddenly tired, suddenly safe, suddenly ready to sleep. My mother rolls over, and soon she is snoring softly.

I close my eyes. Only then do I hear the haunting hiss. I resist the urge to leap up, rush to the safety of my own bed. I can't hide any longer. I reach towards my mother's hair. Tiny bites prick my fingertips. I do not pull away, not even when I feel the venom run through me. Not even when my hand goes numb.

The snoring has stopped. I open my eyes. My mother stares at me, snakes writhing. I stare back, my face a mirror. I wait and wonder, which of us will turn to stone?

Love Lost Found

"We should picnic on the lake," Klara told Oskar. She was getting dressed with her back to him. He lay in bed, down covers pulled over him. It was Sunday. He was looking forward to staying in and watching the Dortmund vs. Leipzig match on TV. They may be living north of Berlin, but he grew up in Leipzig and was a life-long fan.

Klara sat on the bed. She reached under the covers to place a hand on his bare shoulder. Her fingers were cold but quickly warmed. "Come on, it'll be fun. Like it used to be."

At that, Oskar pulled back the covers, smiled at his wife. He sat up and gave her a kiss, the soccer game all but forgotten. Before they were married, and both lived with their parents, they would go to the park for privacy. They would bring along some food and a bottle of wine, but rarely finish either. They would wander into the nearby woods and make love in the gray light filtering through the trees. The fear of getting caught by a policeman on patrol or a group of elderly hikers only added to the excitement. If their parents noticed how dirty their clothes were when the couple returned, they never mentioned it.

After the rush of their wedding and a honeymoon on Santorini, they settled into a nice but affordable refurbished East German tenement. With the ability to have sex whenever they wanted, without ending up with leaves in their hair and sore backs from the rough ground, the excitement quickly wore off. Klara became absorbed in pursuing her doctorate, something about soil erosion Oskar only half understood. He commuted by train into Berlin for work, ninety minutes both ways including his bike ride to the station. Neither had much energy for sex when they got home, even when they did have the time.

KLARA PACKED COLD SAUSAGE, cheese, and dark rye in a rucksack while Oskar filled his bike's saddlebags with bottles of beer. The old road from their flat was narrow and winding, closed in by stone walls and wood fences. Their tires rattled over the cobblestone as they rode through town, past white stucco buildings with red tile roofs. Church bells interrupted the Sunday silence. Shops were closed. People were spending their day with their families or puttering in their gardens. In the town's center, the sun shined bright, almost hot for an early autumn day. The previous spring, the trees that had survived two wars—one hot, one cold—had to be cut down due to disease. The trees planted in their place were still no more than saplings. Everyone in town complained about the lack of shade.

On the other side of town sat the lake. It wasn't a large lake, but it was clear and clean and still as ice. They turned onto the gravel path which circumnavigated it and passed an old woman on a park bench, a gaggle of geese that paid no attention to them. Four teenage boys loitering on the path made space for them as they pedaled by.

They stopped at the hill where they used to picnic before they were married, just a rise in the otherwise flat landscape. Setting down their bikes, they walked up the slope with their picnic in hand. Klara laid a blanket in the shade of a beech tree. Across the lake, they could see an ornate building, long and low. As an architect, Oskar always admired it, even though his tastes favored a more industrial style. He appreciated the arched windows, the gently sloping roof, the perfect symmetry. It had been built as a military officer school in the days of Prussian kings. The Nazis had used it to train Hitler Youth, and the Soviets as a place where sol-diers—dutifully guarding East Germany's borders from an evil West—could come for R & R. Now, it was part of the University where Klara did her lab work and taught biology to underclassmen.

Oskar opened a couple of beers, anxious at the thought of getting his wife a little bit drunk before they made love. Klara had brought reusable plates and silverware, loaded one of the plates with the food she had packed. She was, in almost every way, a modern woman. She was smart and independent. She had been arrested once for protesting nuclear power before the country had decided to abandon it. She was constantly after her school's administration, demanding equal pay for women. Yet she cared for Oskar like some traditional Haus-frau: ironing his shirts, making his lunch in the mornings, having dinner ready when he got home. When they first got married, he protested, told her she didn't need to do those things. She silenced him with a kiss. "I don't do these things because I have to, but because I want to."

Except for the lack of intimacy, she was the perfect wife. He often wondered to himself, as he saw young women stroll the Berlin streets on his way to and from his office if it was enough.

A two-person sailboat glided by, followed a few moments later by a kayaker, oars cutting through the pristine waters. Other than that, the lake was empty. They ate without saying much. The food was simple but good, reminding Oskar of his youth, just after reunification, when capitalism had cured the constant shortages of even the most basic items, and the future was full of hope.

Halfway through the meal and on his second bottle of beer, Oskar leaned in to kiss his wife. She kissed him back.

They made out like teenagers until he couldn't stand it any longer. He gripped her hand, started to lead her into the nearby woods.

"Not here," she said.

"But I thought—"

"Maybe tonight, in our own bed," she replied, but he knew that after that long bike ride back, she would be too tired, and would remind him that they both had to get up early the next morning.

She must have seen the disappointment on his face. "Still, a walk would be nice ," she said.

They packed up the remainder of their food, scraped their dishes, and folded up the blanket, leaving the spot beneath the tree like they had never been. They strolled further up the hill, holding hands. Klara leaned against Oskar, slightly buzzed. He still hoped he could lead her into the woods, began to slowly nudge her in that direction, when she pointed and let out the same little squeak she made when she found something interesting on social media, or an item in a shop she liked.

Oskar looked to where she was pointing. Below them was a small pond, an offshoot of the lake, marshy and green with moss and tall grass. A car partially jutted from the water, its hood a dull beige.

After her initial surprise, Klara's scientific curiosity took over. She clambered down the hill, still holding Oskar's hand, dragging him along with her. She stopped at the pond's edge, as near to the car as they could get. Two round headlights stared at them from just above the waterline like the eyes of a giant frog looking to the sky for its next meal.

"It's an old Trabant," Oskar said. The East German cars, two-cycle, exhaust spewing and completely unreliable, were abandoned by the thousands when the Wall came down. The West wouldn't allow them on their roads for not being able to meet safety and emission standards.

"It looks like it's been here for decades," Klara speculated.

"How come nobody noticed it before?" Oskar asked. "Why hasn't it rotted away?" He had read that the old cars were partially built of plant-based materials, steel being in short supply.

"It's been such a dry, hot summer. The water level is lower than it's ever been. It's possible the marsh kept it preserved. I'd have to test the water to make sure." Klara's eyes gleamed with the excitement of a new area of research. The way they used to gleam for him, he thought. Oskar pulled off his shoes and socks, unbuttoned his shirt. Klara asked him what he was doing.

"You research your way, I'll research mine."

She shrugged, kicked off her sandals and rolled up her pants legs. They waded in together, holding hands for balance. The water was cold, but not freezing. Exploration, a new adventure. A lump formed in Oskar's throat. His heart skipped a beat.

They reached the car. Oskar rocked it to see if it would budge, but it was firmly set in the pond's muddy bottom. Klara made her way around it, tapping it here and there as if hopping someone might knock back. The front windshield was covered in scum. Oskar wiped it clean with his hand. He and Klara peered inside.

The body in the passenger's seat stared at them with hallow eyes, its mouth partly open, seemingly amused.

They both took a step back and composed themselves before leaning forward to inspect the body through the safety of the windshield. Like the car, it had been preserved, or at least partly so. It was a woman as far as they could tell. Flesh still clung to her face, what was left of her hair was done up in a bun. Her hands were behind her back, as if tied there. A wool jacket clung to her decomposing frame.

Oskar went to the passenger side of the car, reached into the water to find the latch. "We've come this far," he told Klara.

To his surprise, the door opened easily. He reached towards the body, ready to pull away should it decide to reach back.

In her jacket, Oskar found a leather ID holder. It almost fell apart in his hands. He waded back to Klara, who stood in front of the car with her arms crossed. They inspected it together. The ID inside was soaked and eaten away at the edges. They could not make out her name, or anything else about her. The ink had faded, unreadable. The photo was also faded but still clear enough to reveal a woman nearing middle age with high cheekbones, a tiny nose, deep set eyes.

"Pretty," Oskar dared.

"I don't think she'd be your type," Klara said. He was right. The ID wasn't a driver's license or a passport, but the ID of the Stasi, the old East German Secret Police.

The Stasi made the Gestapo and the KGB look like pre-school teachers. Oskar had an uncle who they watched night and day for three weeks just because a West German couple had stopped him on the street to ask directions.

They decided it was time to call the police. Four uniforms showed up in short order, followed by two detectives. Not long after, a TV van appeared. Sundays were always slow news days.

Oskar and Klara told their story to the detectives, then to the TV reporter. Onlookers appeared, standing behind a police line with their phones held high. A tow truck came to pull the car from the water. The coroner arrived and zipped the dead woman into a body bag before driving her away.

It was getting dark by the time all was said and done. An officer offered them a ride home, put their bikes in his patrol car, back wheels sticking out.

OSKAR AND KLARA LAY IN BED THAT NIGHT. Oskar scrolled through his phone in hopes that they were trending. Klara was on her laptop, searching for anything about the woman.

"Nothing," she said.

"She died before the internet," Oskar replied. "Besides, we don't even know her name."

"Do you think it was an accident?" There was a lilt in her voice. The thrill of the afternoon still had not worn off.

Oskar shook his head. There were some local stories on the feeds about the body, nothing more. He and Klara were only identified as a couple of young hikers. "The car couldn't have gone that far off the road. No, someone killed her, drove the car there to hide the evidence."

"Other Stasi?"

Oskar shrugged. "Or it happened after East Germany fell and it was someone seeking payback."

"Too bad we're not writers. It would make a great story."

They stayed glued to their screens for a time. At one point, Karla placed a hand on Oskar's thigh, caressed it gently. Setting their devices aside, they embraced, made love beneath the covers. Klara buried herself in his shoulder, bit him lightly. She threw her head back on the pillow again and again. It was over sooner than he would have liked.

It wasn't until afterwards, as she lay with her head on his chest, that he realized it was not him, but the finding of the body that aroused her. He tried not to let it bother him, drifted off to sleep. In his dreams, he felt a hand between his legs. Not Klara's hand, but the dead woman's hand, half rotted away. She stared at him with empty eyes.

He woke to the sound of Klara getting out of bed. He reached out to her, hoping to bring her back to him, felt nothing but the ghost white of rumpled sheets.

The Shape of Things

The Mold-O-Rama stood in the vestibule of the elephant house, a handwritten out-of-order sign taped over its coin slot. Lyle stood in front of it, his gray overalls smeared with grease, his tool bag in his hand. He breathed deep. The building reeked of manure and musk. Only the additional odor of heated plastic could make the experience complete.

The machine looked like a jukebox made from Robbie the Robo spare parts. A clear plastic dome covered the area where a song selector would be, revealing tubes and pipes and gauges. Above the dome, behind an acrylic panel, the statue of an African elephant was displayed next to the words:

Make Your Own Exclusive Product
Molded in Plastic in Seconds
Only $1.00

A few zoo visitors stopped to watch Lyle as he set down his bag, unplugged the machine, and pulled it away from the wall: a woman with an infant in a stroller, a man with a small girl on his shoulders, three pre-teenage boys in baggy shorts and worn high-top sneakers. They looked on with idle fascination as Lyle opened up the back of the machine and examined its inner workings with the small flashlight he kept in his left breast pocket. He paid no attention to those watching him as he went through the trouble-shooting checklist in his head—pressure gauge at ninety pounds, pressure switch on side of the air tank functioning, switch on Number 1 Relay open, coin mechanism settings correct…

He reviewed twenty-two items before locating the problem. The check valve leading from the air compressor to the air tank had to be replaced. He rummaged in his bag and found the valve he needed. He hefted it in his hand and sighed again. It was his last one. He had tried substituting it with modern equivalents, but they just didn't fit right. As with most of the parts in the fifty-year-old machine, only the originals would do.

A half-hour later, Lyle had the new valve in place. He screwed on the back panel and plugged in the machine. Its lights came on. The visitors who had initially stopped to watch him had become bored and moved on a while ago, but as he pulled four quarters out of his pocket and placed them in the coin slot one by one, a new crowd gathered. Children stood on their tiptoes and placed their hands on the machine. It began to hum, and the needles on the air and tank pressure gauges began to climb. The parents stood behind the kids craning their necks to catch a glimpse of the machine at work.

Beneath the dome, pistons drove the two halves of the mold together in the center of the machine. From below, a pipe pumped polyethylene heated to two hundred and fifty degrees into the bottom of the mold. The children scrunched their noses at the acrid smell of hot plastic as another pipe pushed cold air in from the top of the mold, ensuring the plastic filled every nook and cranny. Automotive antifreeze ran through black rubber hoses and into the mold to cool it. After a few moments, the halves of the mold separated, and the plastic model of an African elephant, just like the one on display, slid down into the slot at the bottom of the machine. Lyle picked it up. It was still warm, its features rough and imperfect. A small girl wearing a polka-dot sundress with the string of a blue helium balloon wrapped around her wrist stared wide-eyed. Lyle held it out to her. She took it hesitantly and smiled. Other children reached out to touch it as if it were some holy relic. It gave Lyle hope to see that in this digital age, children could be so enamored with a simple toy created by what amounted to an oversized pressure cooker.

Lyle pretended not to watch as the children *oohed* and *aahed* at the elephant. He found that parents looked at him suspiciously if he took too much interest. Still, he watched them out of the corner of his eye. He loved children. They were always excited, always in awe. For them, everything was new. There was an innocence about them that he relished, mainly because it could so easily be lost.

LYLE TOOK A SHORTCUT through the elephant house to the opposite entrance. The house was wide, with cages on either side, their iron bars reaching from the concrete floor to the high, arched ceiling. Most of the elephants were out in the yard, so the house was relatively quiet. Lyle could hear the echo of his footsteps as he walked. Soon, the elephant house would be empty for good. Slowly but surely, the zoo had been eliminating these antiquated houses and replacing them with more naturalistic exhibits, designed to look like the animals' habitats in the wild. Already the apes, big cats, and tropical birds had been moved into such homes. In a few months, the elephant exhibit would be ready, and this building would become an empty shell, awaiting demolition.

Matilda dominated her cage, eating hay out of a large trough. A thick chain was wrapped around her right front leg, the other end buried into the wall. She wasn't allowed outside. Legend was that in her younger days, she attacked and killed a tuba player in the circus to which she belonged. They would have shot her if the zoo hadn't come to her rescue. She was so old and moved so slowly that it was doubtful she would hurt anyone again, but they weren't taking any chances.

Lyle stopped for a moment in front of Matilda, looked deep into her huge black eyes. He wondered what she would do in the new exhibit they were building. Would she be allowed to roam free, and if so, would she even want to, after all these years in a cage? When he asked the zoo administrators, they gave him wide-eyed looks, as if they had never given it any thought. Their looks gave him his answer.

"We're all locked in our own cages," Lyle said aloud. Matilda fanned her ears, lifting her trunk high overhead.

LYLE'S WORKSHOP WAS LOCATED at the far end of the zoo, beyond the veterinary hospital and research labs, in an area off-limits to visitors. It had been converted from one of the garages that once held the zoo's open-topped buses, the ones painted with zebra stripes and leopard spots that toured the exhibits. He had to beg the zoo administrators for a space of his own, and over the years, he had filled it with spare parts from a dozen Mold-O-Rama machines. Coin slots and tubes, dials and gauges, domes and lights lined tall, narrow shelves pieced together from scrap wood. Two machines were still recognizable as such. One used to make an alligator, the other a koala bear. Their domes were off, and wires spilled from behind their back panels. Their molds lay nearby on the ground. Slowly but surely, Lyle had stripped them for parts. Soon, the machines would be no more than empty casings.

Lyle set his tool bag down on his worktable, dug into his tiny fridge, and pulled out a sandwich he had made earlier that morning. Laid out on the table in front of him were the schematics for a machine of his own design. He reviewed them for the umpteenth time, going over the tube connections and electrical schematics to satisfy himself.

The first time he had seen a Mold-O-Rama was in Hollywood of all places. He was just a boy. He, his parents, and his older sister had driven out West to visit their aunt. Outside Gruaman's Chinese theater, a Mold-O-Rama sat to one side, advertising a red plastic replica of the pagoda-like structure for only twenty-five cents. He begged his mother to buy him one, and after much pleading, she gave him a quarter (she thought it looked like junk, and that it would end up in a box back home with dozens of other forgotten toys and games). He dropped the quarter in the slot and pressed his face against the plastic dome as the machine went to work. It hummed and clattered, and his nose filled with the odor of hot plastic. His mother commented on the unpleasantness of the stench, but to him, it was the best smell in the world. Even now, whenever he breathed it in, it brought him back to childhood. When the statue was finished, he stood on the sidewalk outside the theater, holding it and marveling, the same way the girl in the polka-dot dress had done earlier that day. Despite his mother's concern, he kept that souvenir on a bookshelf in his room for years. He still had it in his apartment now, on display on the credenza like it was a priceless family heirloom.

Wolfing down his sandwich, Lyle looked at the two machines he had recently started to dismantle. It bothered him whenever he had to shut one down for good, but he didn't have a choice. These two had broken down and would have taken too many of his spare parts to repair. He had to keep as many of the machines running as possible, and that meant cannibalizing some of the machines to save the rest. Looking over the plans on his worktable one more time, he sighed more heavily than before. He got out his handcart and was about to do the unthinkable. He was about to dismantle a perfectly working machine on purpose.

LYLE HAD ALWAYS BEEN A TINKERER. As a boy, he had pulled apart just about every appliance in the house at least once just to see how it worked. In high school, he had no interest in studying history or English, preferring to ditch those classes and spend the extra time in shop class.

Lyle had been working at the zoo as a maintenance man for less than a year when the Mold-O-Rama that made the mountain gorilla broke down. The company responsible for the machines had long gone bankrupt and stopped servicing them, so it was up to the zoo to keep them running. His boss at the time, Henry—long retired—handed him a photocopied manual and told him to see what he could do. Lyle had jumped at the chance to get his hands on a machine he remembered so fondly from childhood. Within minutes, he'd found a loose wire in the coin mechanism and reattached it. That was fifteen years ago. He had been responsible for the machines ever since. At first, it was only part of his job, but as the machines grew older, broke down more often, and became harder to repair, it quickly grew into a full-time position.

There were nine functioning Mold-O-Ramas remaining in the zoo—elephant, gorilla, penguin, giraffe, panther, dolphin, polar bear, parrot, and walrus. At first, Lyle tried to decide which one had to go by which one he liked least, but that didn't work because he cherished every one. Instead, he decided using logic. Whichever one took in the least money over a two-week period would be the one to get dismantled. He thought that it would be the parrot or the walrus, since these seemed less popular animals. But after the two weeks, he counted up the quarters. To his surprise, the penguin had lost.

It was near closing time. The sun had already sunk behind the old gothic-style animal houses, and the remaining daylight reflecting off the clouds gave the sky an orange hue. Lyle wheeled the handcart into the penguin house. The evening was warm but the air inside was frigid, even in the vestibule. Through the propped open doors, he could see the large glass cases inside, behind which various species of penguins waddled around a faux-tundra landscape. A young couple stood in front of the glass, a stroller holding a toddler between them. The parents pointed and the child laughed as a penguin dove into the water, swam in circles for a few moments, then waddled out, beads of water flying from his feathers as he shook himself dry.

Lyle watched the young couple and thought of Julie and Andrew. The life that should have been. He shuddered, remembering the day Andrew was born and had died, Julie forced to deliver an infant who did not have a heartbeat. An infant who would never draw a breath. Afterward a nurse took a photo of the three of them together. Their only photo as a family. He and Julie smiling sad but brave smiles, Andrew so peaceful with his eyes closed, his fragile body all clean and pale, so that if Lyle didn't know any better, he would have thought the baby was asleep.

Julie took that photo with her when she left two years later. The doctor told them they could try again, but Julie said she didn't know if she could go on if there was another stillbirth. Their marriage had always been strong, full of love and friendship and a genuine concern for each other. But with Andrew's death, a rift formed between them. When Julie left, it broke Lyle's heart, but he understood when she told him, "Every time I look at you, I'm reminded of Andrew. It hurts too much."

Lyle had never given up hope that he and Julie could reconcile. They had been high school sweethearts. She was the only one he ever wanted—ever *would* want. If not for Andrew's death, they could have lived together to a ripe old age, as he had always dreamed.

As the couple wheeled their stroller out the door, they nodded and smiled at Lyle. For a moment, he wondered if they knew what he was about to do. He shook his head. How could they? And even if they did know, who were they to approve or disapprove? Unlike Matilda, he was going to break out of his cage.

Lyle unplugged the machine and threw a blanket over it. Lifting one end, he slid the hand truck beneath it and leaned it backward. Carefully, he wheeled it outside and down the short flight of stairs. A few of the zoo staff and visitors who still lingered watched him as he passed them on his way to his workshop.

IN HIS WORKSHOP, LYLE REMOVED the pipe that dispensed the plastic into the mold. He cleaned it out with a pipe cleaner, blowing through it to make sure it was clear. Covered by a canvas tarp in the back of the shop was the machine, a year in the making, consistent with the plans on his worktable. It was larger than the others. It had no coin slot, no display. It didn't light up, but it had all that it needed to shape the plastic, including a mold he had created himself that was several times larger than the normal mold and one hundred times more detailed. This meant that he needed to have a lot of liquid injected into the mold quickly before it cooled, and that meant a second and third pipe. When he found that he didn't have any spares amongst his menagerie of parts, he had no choice but to take from a working Mold-A-Rama. He looked over at the penguin machine. It still saddened him to have to disconnect it, but if this worked, it would all be worth it.

Lyle installed the new pipe and checked the seams for leaks. He leaned in towards the two halves of the mold he had created. He ran his fingers along them, felt every nook and cranny, every curve and line. Finally, it was ready. He said a prayer. He had faith in his abilities as a mechanic, and that the machinery was in working order, but that wasn't the problem. There was a lot that went into the machine of which he had only a rudimentary understanding, ancient knowledge gleaned from forgotten tomes off library shelves, ingredients gathered from remote fields or bought in shops he didn't know existed until he went looking for them.

It grew dark quickly this time of year. For a moment, Lyle wondered if he shouldn't wait. Maybe he should go home and get a good night's sleep. Do this in the light of day. But he waited this long, and he didn't want to wait any longer.

Lyle's hand trembled as he plugged in the machine. He stepped back, the two halves of the mold came together, and the pipes began to inject the liquid into it. Not unexpectedly, the size of the machine made it slightly unstable. It rattled and clunked, but it was doing its job.

From within the mold, Lyle smelled hot flesh and heard the muffled cries of a newborn babe.

Buck Fever

The two brothers pulled up the winding gravel drive to what they always referred to as their father's cabin, even though their father had died three years ago and it, along with several surrounding acres, belonged to them now. It sat in a slight recess, surrounded by woods, hidden from the highway. The brothers talked about clearing away some of the trees that grew closest to the cabin in case of a forest fire, but always seemed to have better things to do.

Ray got out from the driver's side of the rusting Ford Bronco while Jimmy hopped out of the front passenger seat. They carried their rifles in canvas cases. Ray slung his old army duffle over his shoulder and grabbed the cooler from the back, while Jimmy took out his tote and a box of groceries.

The old door creaked as Ray unlocked the heavy padlock and they went inside. They opened the windows, the cool late autumn air wiping away the musty smell that always developed whenever they were gone for more than a couple weeks. They set their bags, along with their rifles, in the one bedroom. Jimmy put the box on the kitchen counter, removed a pot and set it on the propane burner.

"Della made stew," Jimmy said. Hunks of beef, carrots, and potatoes swam in rich gravy. "Said she didn't want us living on beer and beef jerky the whole weekend."

"God bless her," Ray said without irony. He flipped open the cooler and took out two beer bottles.

By the time the stew heated, it was already dark and they'd both downed their first beers. Jimmy knew his brother shouldn't be drinking but couldn't do much to stop him. Still, he promised himself he'd say something after the third one. Ray was a sloppy drunk, sometimes violent, and while Jimmy could hold his own against his big brother, he didn't want it to be that kind of weekend.

Jimmy poured two steaming bowls of stew while Ray shut the windows and started a fire in the wood-burning stove. "Have to call Drake to bring us some more," he said.

"We won't be here that long," Jimmy replied. He plopped down next to his brother on the cracked leather sofa. The bowl was warm in his hands and gave off an aroma that reminded him of when they were teenagers and they'd come in from football practice in rain-soaked jerseys, and their mother would be prepared with fresh towels and something hot on the stove.

Ray seemed to feel it, too. He looked out the window into swiftly approaching dark. "Sometimes, I think I'd like to live up here full-time," he said.

Jimmy shook his head. The cabin may be their second home, but their father never intended for it to be more than a place to crash after a long day hunting or quiet time fishing. It was drafty in winter, hot in summer, no air-conditioning and only the wood stove for heat.

"Tina would never go for it," Jimmy said.

"Yeah, well, soon she may not be in the picture."

"Still bad, huh?"

"As ever," Ray replied. Tina was his second wife.

After a messy divorce, Jimmy wondered why his brother had gotten remarried. He asked him about it once. "Man shouldn't be alone," he had said.

"Wish I could have what you and Della have," he now said.

"I got lucky. Be with her till the day I die if she'll have me."

"Be a fool not to."

Jimmy was surprised at this rare compliment from his brother, this big guy with close cropped hair who as a boy would tease him mercilessly, bully him incessantly. Jimmy always wanted to hang out with Ray, but Ray wouldn't have a kid cramping his style, making him look silly in front of the pretty girls who used to come around. It wasn't until much later, when Ray got out of the military, their mother had passed away, and their father's cancer had worsened, that they started coming to the cabin.

A semi rumbled down the highway. A tanker truck making its way from the fracking fields up north. They could hear it a half mile off.

Jimmy produced a third beer for each of them from the cooler, determined this would be Ray's last. He twisted off the caps and they sat in the orange glow of the stove. They got into an argument about which was better, Ray's Remington .30-06 or Jimmy's .358 Winchester. In the end, they agreed to disagree.

"Still no substitute for an M24," Ray said. He'd been a sniper in the army.

"A bit of overkill," Jimmy replied.

"Depends on what you're hunting," Ray replied. He started on his fourth beer. Jimmy joined him, not saying a word.

THE BROTHERS WOVE BETWEEN THE TREES, walking side by side a few yards apart. Jimmy cradled his rifle so that the muzzle was pointed away from his brother. Ray carried his with the barrel pointed downwards, finger near but not on the trigger, the way a soldier would.

The air was crisp. The leaves had turned from brilliant orange, ochre and red to dull shades of brown. Some still clung to their branches, but most covered the forest floor, crunching beneath their boots.

The brothers reached the deer stand—a wood enclosure raised on stilts twenty feet up. They climbed the ladder, rungs evenly spaced, Ray taking the lead. He popped open the trap door, sliding over to make way for Jimmy, who followed close behind. Jimmy noted that a section of the roof was rotting out, and would start leaking if it wasn't fixed soon. Over the past three years, the two brothers had replaced every board in the stand at least once as the driving rains and heavy snows took their toll. Jimmy sometimes considered replacing it with a sturdier, manufactured metal and fiberglass model designed to withstand the elements but would never bring this up to Ray. Their father had built this stand, carefully placing it so that the trees would hide it, but at the same time, provide a line of site in every direction. He brought each of them here as soon as they were old enough to hold a rifle. Jimmy had been to his father's grave a couple of times and felt nothing, but he couldn't come through the stand's trap door without sensing his father's presence, the big man with a soft voice, gently instructing them on how to take aim, how to squeeze the trigger.

In silence, they loaded their rifles, took their traditional spots. There were openings on all four sides. Jimmy looked to the east, towards the cabin. Ray peered through binoculars to the west, beyond the woods into a field of tall, dying grass intersected by the highway, its asphalt like black water. Until last year, the highway had been a lonely gravel road, used occasionally by fellow hunters and the adventurous few looking for a remote spot to hike or camp. During the construction that paved and widened it to accommodate the trucks from the fracking fields, the noise from the bulldozers, dump trucks, jackhammers and steamrollers scared away most of the animals. The two brothers shot nothing that season.

It was early. The highway was nearly empty. A jeep with kayaks on the roof went by, but that was all. Ray took a thermos from the backpack he carried. He poured hot coffee into the cap which served as a lid, offered it to his brother. Jimmy waved it away. He could smell the whiskey. He expected it was as much alcohol as it was coffee.

"Last night was one thing," he said, ashamed he'd said nothing the night before about his brother's drinking. "But out here, with our guns? Not smart." He thought of their buddy Erik, who got so drunk he shot himself in the foot, and their cousin Frazier who nearly put a bullet through his son's head, but luckily just grazed the skull.

"My choice, little brother. Back in the desert, you couldn't get a drink if you tried, and I tried. Would have helped take the edge off." He took a sip. "They can teach anyone how to shoot. That's the easy part. Look Dad even taught you," Ray said. Jimmy didn't argue. He had been awkward as a boy, still was in some ways. He couldn't catch a football, couldn't hit a fastball. It took him forever to get his aim straight. The first time he took a shot at a deer, he was thirteen. Despite all his father had taught him, his hands shook, he couldn't breathe. The shot went wide.

"No, it's not the shooting," Ray continued, referring to his time in the service. He rarely talked about it, but the therapist told him that when he did, Jimmy should let him talk. At one point, the therapist advised Jimmy to take all his brother's guns away. He couldn't bring himself to do it. Besides, like Ray told him, if he really wanted to do himself in, he could get a gun as easily as he could buy a hammer. "It's the killing. Being able to pull the trigger, knowing you're taking someone's life, even if the son-of-a-bitch does deserve it. *That* you can't teach. You just have to be able to do it."

Jimmy nodded knowingly. He thought about the first time he bagged a buck a year after that disastrous first attempt. Afterwards, his dad took him to a corner tavern for a beer. He sat at the lacquered table, sick to his stomach. Whether it was from the bitter taste of beer or the memory of the buck lying dead, black eyes open, he couldn't be sure. He didn't say anything to his father, who sat across from him brimming with pride.

The brothers settled into a long silence with no sign of even a doe or a stray fawn. A rabbit hopped through the tall grass. The brothers ignored it. Their rifles would have blown it to smithereens, but it wasn't the prey they were looking for. The highway traffic was still light. A couple of pick-up trucks, nothing more.

"Some guys at the gas station in town say that fracking's been good for business," Jimmy said to break the quiet. Town meant Devan, about five miles to the south, five hundred people and shrinking fast. "Some of the younger folks are staying to work there, instead of going to one of the big cities."

"Good for business." Ray spat the words. "What would Dad say about that?"

"I'm not arguing," Jimmy replied. "Just saying what people think."

"People think a lot of things. There's an invisible man in the sky who gives a crap about us, if you ask most of them. Doesn't make it true."

A young buck appeared out of the trees. A six-pointer. He stood in the tall grass, head turned towards the highway. At the same moment, a semi came around the bend—red cab, silver tanker, exhaust filling the blue sky with white smoke, deceptively clean. The speed limit was fifty-five, but like most vehicles, it was doing eighty, easy.

The buck was on Ray's side of the blind, but he tapped his brother on the shoulder, motioned for him to take the shot.

Jimmy tried to say no thanks with a motion of his hand, but Ray was having none of it, he grabbed his brother by his vest, moved him into position.

Resting his rifle on the sill, Jimmy peered through the scope. The buck twitched his ears as the semi barreled down the road. The driver had both hands on the wheel, a week's growth of white beard and a sweat stained cap.

For a moment, Jimmy was that thirteen-year-old boy again, hunting with his father. His heart raced. He trembled. He sweat despite the cold. He recalled the black eyes of that first buck he killed, considered pulling back, not taking the shot.

A hand fell on his shoulder. It was Ray's but could have just as easily have been his father's. Jimmy couldn't let either of them down.

He took several deep breaths to calm himself. His hands held steady. As the semi was almost even with the buck, the deer turned his head, looked about to spring away. Jimmy fired.

The buck took off with the boom of the rifle, disappearing into the woods. The semi driver slumped over the wheel. The tanker truck careened, skidding into the culvert, jackknifing so that its chassis faced the brothers, wheels still spinning.

Ray slapped Jimmy on the back as Jimmy went limp. "Nice shot," Ray said. He handed Jimmy the cup from the thermos. Jimmy drank. It burned his throat, the aftertaste bitter and lingering. "You get used to it," Ray said, and poured his brother some more.

The Lonely Box

Loneliness lurked just beyond the workbench shop light, watching as Jeff sawed and glued and nailed. He was no carpenter, but he considered himself handy, having renovated most of his century-old home himself. Still, a box was different. The sides had to be accurately measured and cut, the lid fitted so that it would close properly, could keep anything sealed inside from getting out. The last thing Jeff wanted was for his loneliness to escape.

His phone played a selection of seventies rock to keep him company—Chicago, the Eagles, the Allman Brothers. Bands he'd listened to in high school, playing on the radio as he cruised with his buddies in his dad's lime green LTD, when he thought life would last forever and he was never, ever alone.

His friends were gone. Darren died of an aneurysm at the age of forty-one. Greg lived nearby but was always busy with his new wife and a young son. Rick lived in Seattle and it had been years since they spoke. Now, the music, those memories, and working on the box were all that kept his loneliness at bay.

Finally complete, he inspected his work. The joints were tight, but the hinges took some adjustment to get the box to seal. He opened and shut the lid a couple of times, flipped the latch. Not perfect, but good enough.

He took the box into the yard along with a spade. His loneliness followed at a distance, drawing nearer with each step, black against the night. Above him, the bedroom light was on, filtered through lace curtains. Janet was no doubt in her usual spot, on her side of the bed, pillows propping her up and the TV turned to some old rerun. She didn't bother to ask him what he was doing in the garage that late. She didn't bother to talk to him much at all anymore. He could not say when they grew apart. It happened gradually—dinner by dinner, conversation by conversation, until, one day, he realized they were living separate lives.

The rest of the house was dark. Erik and Sonia's rooms were almost the way they'd left them when they finally moved out on their own, one after the other. Sometimes, he found himself sitting on their beds, replaying conversations from their younger days in his head. They spoke now and then over the phone, but it wasn't the same.

Jeff set the box on the patio table. If he had taken the time, he could have sanded it, maybe given it a coat of leftover varnish. It's not like he didn't have the time. Since his retirement, he had nothing but time. Raising his children, working at his job, even renovating the house had all given him purpose. Those days, he longed to be able to rest. Now, he only wished the resting would stop.

The dog next door barked. His neighbor—Cliff or Clive, he could never remember—called the dog inside. He was a widower. He had a telescope that he sometimes took out on clear nights. Other than that, Jeff knew little about the man. Over the years, they'd exchanged waves and hellos, but that was about it. There was a gate between the two houses. Who had built it and why, Jeff didn't know. It seemed it had always been there. Perhaps, once, the people in these houses had been friends, maybe even family. The gate hadn't been used in a long time.

Jeff could feel loneliness at his back, still lurking, ready to envelop him. The idea of a box to keep it in came to him as he was doing a long-delayed chore. He had the habit of saving the original packaging for anything he bought long after the item had broken or become obsolete and taken to recycling. Boxes for old toasters, TVs, mixers, and computers cluttered a quarter of his basement. Janet had been nagging him to get rid of them, and he figured he might as well. He had nothing else to do.

As he whiled away an afternoon flattening all those boxes in a neat stack, he thought about how he kept the boxes in case he needed to return the items kept in them. He no longer had these items. Yet, he had his loneliness, and it had to go back. Why shouldn't it have a box as well? But not some piece of reused cardboard. No, that wouldn't do. If it was to work, the box would have to be of his own making.

His loneliness crept onto his shoulders as he knew it would, as it always did when he was still, its emptiness a great weight that made it difficult to move. But move he did. He spun, snatching it before it could react, catching it unaware. It tingled in his hands as he shoved it into the box and shut the lid tight, latching it quickly so it wouldn't escape.

In Janet's garden, where tomatoes and carrots were just beginning to sprout, he found a spot to bury the box. He dug deeper than he needed to, setting a large rock on top it just for good measure. He refilled the hole and tamped the soil down with the back end of the spade before setting it aside.

He looked up. He used to be able to read the sky when he was young and people still dreamed of reaching the moon. He could name each constellation, had known a planet from a star by how it failed to twinkle. Jeff thought about his neighbor with his telescope. He went to the gate. It was covered in vines and the latch was almost rusted shut. He had to put all his weight into it to get it open.

The dog barked from inside. A light came on. His neighbor stepped onto the porch and asked who it was. Jeff answered to the man, the moonlight, the shadow that was not there.

How to Protect Your Child

W*omen must never be left alone during the first few weeks following childbirth, for madness has more power over them.*

Jessie slept in fits and starts between feedings. She would nod off for minutes at a time, perhaps as much as a half hour, Alex still at her breast. Sometimes she even dared to dream.

...It is spring, the sun warm, flowers finally in bloom. Alex—no longer a newborn, too-soon a toddler—runs toward her through the tall grass, each precarious step a controlled fall. His gold curls, impossibly long, flow down below his shoulders. His outstretched hand holds a bouquet of dandelions. He laughs. He trips over his own feet. Jessie reaches out, fails to catch him as he drowns in a sea of green...

Jessie woke with a start. She had fallen asleep sitting up in her grandmother's old wingback. Alex dozed in her arms, swaddled tight, face warm against her naked bosom. His rosebud lips moved as if still nursing. A tuft of black hair peaked out from under his cap. Jessie had been born with that same black hair. Before she turned one, it had all fallen out, replaced by blond tresses.

On the other side of the living room, Alex's empty cradle swayed. Jessie rose and went to the cradle, bracing herself against the faded arm of the chair as she clung to Alex with the other, cringing as her episiotomy stitches stretched.

The cradle had been hers, and before that, her mother's—built by her grandfather in the workshop adjoining the barn. He had found it stored in the loft, covered with a moth-eaten Afghan, dark stain faded. Cleaning it up the best she could, she placed it in the living room beneath the iron floor grate, where it could be warmed by oil fueled heat pumped straight up from the cellar. She had yet to place Alex in it, though. She wouldn't dare let him go.

Melted snow pooled beneath the cradle. A thick handprint smudged one of its top rails. The front window drapes, laced with flowers and twenty years out of fashion, were partly open. Jessie strained to recall whether or not she had closed them earlier that evening.

The moon shone full and bright through icy panes. Snow blew across the hard, flat landscape forming deep drifts against the barn not twenty yards away. Across the road, a pickup truck was parked on the shoulder, a later model, silent and dark. It had not been there earlier that day. Jessie reached for her phone, dialed 911. David had always been fond of old trucks.

JESSIE MOVED ABOUT THE HOUSE making sure all the windows and doors were locked. The operator said she would send a police car out, but she didn't know when it would be there. With the sub-zero temperatures there were a lot of people stranded in their cars or at home without heat, she said. The volunteer firefighters were stretched to the limit. The police were picking up the slack. The operator's voice was calm, controlled. Jessie imagined her to be heavy set, middle-aged, settled in her life. In her tone, Jessie could hear the underlying question she was too polite to ask, "Why was a young woman living in the middle of nowhere, in the dead of winter, all alone with a newborn child? She should be with family, with friends. Where was the child's father?"

How could she explain what she, herself, barely understood? She had walked out on David when she was seven months pregnant because no matter how much he said he wanted to be a father, it didn't matter. It didn't matter that he painted his office a bright yellow and turned it into a nursery. It didn't matter that he had given up hunting trips to go to the ultrasound appointments. She knew, in the end, he would leave them. He never finished college, hadn't had a job for more than nine months. He spent money as fast as he earned it, when he earned anything at all. Jessie's own father had left before she turned two years old. She had no memory of him, apart from the legacy of the effect his leaving had on her mother. She did not want to end up like that. No, better to leave than to be left.

And when Jessie had decided to run away, what better place to go than the home where she was raised by her grandparents? She didn't sell it after her grandmother finally passed away and willed it to her. Instead, she paid a local company that mainly maintained summer homes in winter to care for it. As if even before David, even before Alex, she knew she would one day need sanctuary.

The day she brought Alex home from the hospital, David called her. He threatened to get a lawyer and sue for custody. Jessie laughed. As if he had the money for an attorney. She was the one who had been supporting the both of them designing firewalls. Her laughter was met with silence, then the slam of the phone on the other end.

Alex stirred. He blinked open his eyes, grunted softly. Jessie lifted him up and carried him to her grandmother's wingback. She kissed him on his forehead—elongated from being pushed out of the womb—and unbuttoned her blouse and brought him to her breast. He sucked hard. Jessie's eyes welled up as she realized that Alex was her life now. She had left David, left her job, and although she could freelance, she couldn't do it here without a connection to the web. Besides, she couldn't concentrate long enough to remember what day it was, let alone string together a line of code to keep hackers at bay.

Jessie recalled long days carrying over into night as she became lost in her work, pizza at one a.m., waking up late to make love to David while the mid-morning sun seeped through the blinds. That was when there was still love between them. She didn't know which made her feel worse—a life lost or the guilt that came from missing it. Wasn't she supposed to love her child more than anything in the world, find a new joy to surpass all others? She held Alex tight, stopped short of gripping him too hard.

Women who have recently delivered must not go to sleep until someone is watching over the child. Mothers who are overcome by sleep often have changelings laid in their cradles.

THE TRUCK STILL SAT BETWEEN the road and the culvert. Snow blew against it, settling around its tires. It had been over an hour since Jessie had called 911. There was no way of knowing when, or *if*, the police would come.

Jessie bowed her head against the biting wind, Alex warm beneath her coat, snuggled in a sling across her chest. Snow reflected the moonlight, crunched beneath her feet. It was safer in the house, Jessie knew. But she had to be sure it wasn't just David she needed to worry about. Besides, there was nothing to do inside but wait and try to ward off sleep.

Jessie scanned the truck with a flashlight. Its bed was filled with bags of sand and rock salt, no doubt to keep the old rear wheel drive from fishtailing on the icy roads. The cab was empty except for a travel mug nestled between the seats. Jessie put her palm over the hood. The engine was cold.

Noises like tiny branches breaking came from the woods. Footprints in the snow made a wide arc, heading towards the house before disappearing beyond the trees. The footprints had been eroded by the wind. They appeared small, like a child's.

She followed them to the woods and stopped. She stretched out her foot as if testing the water of a pond in early spring. For the first time since she was a young girl, she stepped among the trees of the woods.

JESSIE WAS ONLY TEN YEARS OLD when her mother dropped her off with her grandmother and said good-bye. It was less than a year since her grandfather had died and the house looked in good repair, as if he was still around to care for it—porch floorboards that didn't sag near the door, fresh paint, new shingles, a vegetable garden ripe with summer squash, tomatoes, leaf lettuce, and snow peas.

Jessie's mother told her daughter she was sick, that she was going to the hospital to get better and would come back soon. Jessie could tell when her mother was lying, knew she was never coming back. Standing with her grandmother on the gravel drive, she watched her mother drive away in her rusted-out Olds. Jessie's grandmother smiled down at Jessie, her eyes bright behind thick bifocals. She took the young girl's hand in her own age spotted one, bony fingers frail. Jessie pulled away. Her grandmother reached for her. Jessie turned and ran. She sped through the vegetable garden, past the barn, through the pens where pigs lay in the cool, black-brown mud. Her grandmother called to her in a high, melodic voice, but still, Jessie ran. She did not know this woman. She had met her only a few times before. The last time was at her grandfather's funeral, a day which ended with her and her mother racing off before they even had a chance to grab a sandwich at the church basement reception. Her mother would not have left her here if things were not really bad, worse than when they were kicked out of their apartment, worse than when "Uncle Steve" beat her mother up while Jessie hid beneath the covers in her bed in the next room. She had to get away.

Jessie had ducked into the woods. Sunlight shined bright through boughs thick with green. Underbrush wrapped around her ankles. Spiny weeds pricked her bare legs. She did not stop. She hopped over fallen trees, tripped her way over boulders half sunk in the earth. The thick air stifled her breath. Overhead, unseen birds twittered and trilled. A rabbit dashed across her path.

At the creek, Jessie stopped. Her clothes were soaked with sweat, her throat dry. The creek flowed clean and clear. She wondered if she could drink from it. If it was safe enough to splash onto her face. It was then that she saw the kobold, perched on a thick branch that hung low over the water. Its bloodshot eyes bugged out from a mushroom-shaped head. Its claws dug into the bark. Hairs like thin wire poked from its oversized ears Its flared its nostrils, grinned at her with blackened teeth.

Jessie forgot her fatigue. She tripped her way back through the woods, retracing her steps until she was back at her grandmother's house. All the while, she thought she heard footsteps behind her, imagined hot breath against her nape.

Her grandmother was still waiting on the gravel drive. Jessie fell into her arms. Her grandmother lifted her up, and with strength Jessie didn't know an old woman could have, carried her into the house and laid her on the soft white down of her own bed. The windows were open. Lace curtains blew like angel wings. Lavender scented the air. Her grandmother sat next to her on the edge of the bed, stroked Jessie's hair until she drifted off to sleep.

It wasn't until several days later that her grandmother told her about the kobolds. "What they wanted most," she said, "were beautiful children." Theirs were as ugly as themselves, and so they would exchange them when they were babies and raise the stolen children as their own. She told Jessie the ways to protect a child from being exchanged and what to do if it ever happened. She relayed this to Jessie, not to scare her, but to make her understand that the kobold had no interest in a girl her age—they wanted children they could mold from infancy. She reassured Jessie that there were ways to combat them and promised that they couldn't come into her house for as long as she lived, perhaps longer. The magic that protected her home tended to linger.

Still, even as Jessie grew to be a young woman in her grandmother's house, she never entered the woods after that day. And although she was not raised religious, would cross herself whenever she had to go near it.

NOW, SHE WAS AMONG those trees for the first time since girlhood. They loomed over her, their bare branches grown together like spider webs. The dark trunks blocked the wind, providing some relief from the blowing snow. Jessie straightened. She had Alex bundled in her coat. She followed the footprints with her flashlight. They went into the woods a couple dozen feet or so, and then turned back to the rear of the house. Jessie breathed deep as she stepped back out into the open, even though the cold wind hurt her lungs.

The footprints ended at a cellar window. One of the panes had been busted in. The snow had been cleared away so that the window could be opened. Scanning the cellar with her flashlight, she glimpsed several cardboard boxes, some of her grandmother's old belongings that she would have to go through one day, a half dozen clay pots filled with potting soil, and the rumbling oil furnace.

Jessie swore aloud, her worst fear realized. How stupid she had been to believe that the power of her grandmother's incantations could protect her, not only from the kobold, but from David as well! Who knew if the magic ever existed at all? More than once, at more reasonable times, Jessie laughed them off as nothing more than the maginations of an old woman trying to ease her granddaughter's fears. Jessie had only seen glimpses the magic late at night when she was supposed to be asleep. She would watch from her window while her grandmother stood in the yard below, spreading what looked like talc in a wide arc across the lawn, chanting in a language that Jessie could not understand.

Jessie swayed. She closed her eyes. Her toes, her fingertips, her face were all but frozen. Her eyes popped open, unaware of how long she had been there, ankle deep in the snow. After a moment, she realized that she had fallen asleep standing up. She had never done that before, even when working eighteen hours straight to meet deadline. She hurried inside. If she was to be any use to Alex, she had to rest.

Whenever the mother sleeps, she must lay an article of a man's clothing on the child, so that it cannot be exchanged.

JESSIE OPENED THE DOOR and climbed the creaky, narrow staircase, holding Alex with one hand while bracing against the wobbling handrail with the other. The second floor was so cold Jessie wouldn't have been surprised to find it coated with ice. She had closed it up when she first arrived to save on heat. The rooms were dark, save for shafts of moonlight that broke through half opened curtains. There were two bedrooms. One had two twin beds. The other, the one which had belonged to Jessie when she was young, had a full-sized brass bed with a trundle underneath. Both rooms still had dressers, nightstands, trunks and lamps, faded color photos on the walls. Her grandmother had never been fond of change.

She went through the closets, the trunks, the dressers. They were almost empty. A few musty women's blouses, nothing more. With her free hand, she tossed them all aside.

Then, in the back of the closet in the room with the twin beds, she found what she was looking for. A pair of her grandfather's trousers, splattered with paint. The cuffs were frayed, and a weathered belt was still strung through the belt loops. The smells of paint thinner and the Lucky Strikes he had smoked since the war still lingered. She never knew her grandfather, but her grandmother used to tell stories. "A big, loud man, you could always hear his voice in a crowd," she would say, her face all alight. "He knew the land and worked hard to make it work for him. A good man."

Alex began to wail. Jessie touched his face. It felt like ice. She slung the pants over her shoulder and hurried downstairs. She checked all the windows and doors again, turning the handle of the cellar door twice for good measure. She even checked the chimney flue—it never did shut tight. If she listened closely, she could hear the wind whistle through it, soft and low.

Jessie dragged the wingback so that the back of it braced the cellar door. Pulling the cradle next to it, she placed Alex inside, her fingers lingering a moment before letting him go. She laid the old pair of pants across the cradle and settled into the wingback. She folded her hands in her lap, hummed a lullaby that her grandmother used to hum every night before Jessie went to bed, even after Jessie was too old for it. She wished she could remember the words, something about a meadow, a maiden, and a sheep that knew how to fly. The words had been oddly comforting, had made her feel safe and warm on the coldest nights.

Eventually, her hum faded, her eyes closed, her head sank. It wasn't until a child who was not Alex began to cry that Jessie awoke. She looked in the cradle. The infant flailed its pudgy arms and legs, kicking its burlap blanket away to reveal a crooked body, a flattened face. It looked at Jessie with bulging eyes and screamed, opening its mouth wide to reveal blackened gums.

The drapes billowed. One of the windows was open. Outside, the truck was gone.

If your child is exchanged, take the changeling to the river, and make to drown it. The kobold will respond to its cries by bringing back the exchanged child and taking the beast-child away.

THE CHANGELING WAS WRAPPED in Jessie's coat, searching for her nipple through her sweater. Jessie held its bulbous head tight to keep it still. In the hour or so she had the child, it had done nothing but eat and cry. She tried to console it, but no amount of rocking or lullabies would settle it. She gave it a bottle of milk from what she had pumped earlier that day. It drank it down in a few swallows and screamed even louder. She tried to nurse it, but its mouth was like a vacuum against her already sore nipples, and soon she was dry.

The trees closed around Jessie as she trudged through the woods towards the creek. Throwing the changeling into the water was the only way. But when she reached the creek, she swore. The water was frozen, of course! How could she have not realized it would be? She looked around, as if someone, anyone—the ghost of her grandmother perhaps—would appear and tell her what to do next. No one came, but as the infant cried beneath her coat, she slowly came to realize what she had to do.

Jessie placed the changeling beneath a tall fir and knelt in the snow, digging a hole just wide enough to fit an infant. A hole just deep enough so that, once covered over, no one would hear its dreadful wails. As she dug, she kept looking over her shoulder, expecting the mother to come. When she put the child in, she did so slowly, to give the mother more of a chance to arrive. She began to cover the changeling with snow, starting with its feet, working up to its legs, its stomach, its chest, with each handful. No one came.

Perhaps the mother thought she was bluffing, or perhaps it had been David who had taken Alex, and not the kobold. The truck was gone, after all, and it had to be his. But no, there had to be another explanation for the truck's arrival, and its disappearance. How else to explain the presence of the changeling? She would have to take this a step further. Snow cupped in her hands, she held it over the changeling's face, that hideous, flattened, crying, unlovable face. Rising, Jessie kicked the snow on top of the changeling until the crying was muffled—until it stopped all together.

Perhaps it was for the best, Jessie thought as she made her way back to the house. She was not fit to be a mother. Now her life could return to the way it used to be. Alex was an accident, after all. Perhaps he never should have been. An accident. Yes, that was it. A sweet and happy accident. The kobold knew this and was correcting the mistake.

Jessie stepped out of the woods and was hit with a blinding light. Squinting, she could just make out the silhouette of a state trooper—wide brimmed hat, breeches. The trooper asked Jessie if she was okay. She opened her mouth to answer but found her mouth too dry to speak.

In silence, she led the trooper to the spot where she had buried the changeling. Seeing the snow disturbed at their feet, he guessed what she had done. He stuck his flashlight in the snow and began to dig with his gloved hands while Jessie leaned against a tree, shivering. The trooper dug until he hit the bare, frozen ground. He straightened. He wore wire rim glasses and had the barrel chest of an ex-marine. His face was lined with age. He looked at Jessie as if she were his teenage daughter who had just come home late from curfew and was more than half drunk.

The radio clipped to the trooper's down coat crackled. A man spoke. The trooper replied. Jessie did not hear the conversation. She was finding it as difficult to listen as it was to speak. She looked down into the empty hole, gazed up into the trees.

DURING THE RIDE TO THE SITE of the rollover, Jessie slept—truly slept—and when she awoke, she felt shame. What mother would sleep while her newborn was missing?

The pickup was on its side, several yards before the intersection of County Road T and Route 51. Shattered glass sparkled in the snow like stars.

Two EMTs were wheeling a body on a gurney into an ambulance. The body was wrapped in a body bag. The trooper brought Jessie to it and one of the EMTs unzipped the bag. She saw David's face in the flashing blue and red lights of the ambulance, cut a thousand times with shards of broken windshield. She nodded. The EMT zipped the bag back up.

A second trooper approached from the pickup. He cradled another bag, this one much smaller than the first.

"Alex?" Jessie said in a scratchy whisper.

"We'll have to wait for the autopsy." The second trooper was talking to the one who had brought Jessie as if she wasn't there. He was tall and lanky and spoke in a soft baritone.

"I have to see," Jessie said, voice cracking.

The trooper holding the child shook his head. "No car seat. Baby was thrown from the vehicle. Hit the ground hard, face first. Better to remember him the way he was." He nodded to the gurney with David's body as it was loaded into the ambulance. "Patch of black ice. Guy didn't know how to drive in this weather." The easy answer but not the right one. David was a skilled winter driver, knew enough to weigh down the back of his truck.

Jessie slipped away from the troopers. She wandered to where the tread marks left the road, and the snowbank gave way. She took small, careful steps as so not to slip on the ice the officer had mentioned. But there was no ice, only snowpack providing solid traction. Light footprints, short and wide, led into the darkness. In the distance, she heard a familiar cry.

Children who are exchanged but not returned are raised by the kobolds deep underground. They surface at times and can be seen at village markets stealing fruit. They are often thin and pale, but other than that healthy and well cared for.

HANDS TUCKED DEEP IN THE POCKETS of her grandmother's overcoat, collar up to guard against the autumn chill, Jessie trudged through the woods. She had forced herself to overcome the fear of it.

The ground was thick with leaves, the sun bright but without warmth. She had a satellite dish installed in the spring so that she could have high speed internet and freelance far from the pitying and the curious. She kept the Weather Channel on while she worked to stave off the loneliness. The meteorologists, all smiles, talked about it being a cool autumn. Snow was due as early as the next week.

The soles of Jessie's boots slipped as she walked along the wet embankment of the creek. Twice she almost fell into the water, which ran colder and colder as the days grew short.

Since winter, she had done little but work and walk. Work to keep her mind off Alex. Walk to find some trace of the kobold and her now lost child. The medical examiner did not conduct a DNA test on the baby they believed to be Alex. Why waste the resources? Who else could it have been? Jessie tried to show the troopers the footprints she had seen, but the wind had blown them to nothing by the time they arrived, and the distant cries had stopped. They searched the woods for some sign of the changeling Jessie claimed to have buried but found nothing.

Still, no one could explain the results of the autopsy. The child was already dead before the crash. The official cause of death was suffocation.

"Sometimes, there are no good explanations," the medical examiner told Jessie.

Afterwards, Jessie spent two weeks in the hospital. She was dehydrated, exhausted, her nerves shattered. Even now, she drove an hour to see a therapist once a week and popped anti-depressants to treat what the doctor said was lingering postpartum depression. Only recently was she starting to believe what everyone had been telling her. David had taken Alex, and the changeling was how her subconscious chose to deal with the trauma and the guilt. Only recently was she beginning to stop wishing she were dead.

Still, Jessie walked. Her hope and doubt combined with what had become a habit. She was about to turn back toward the house and return to work when something darted between the trees up ahead, too big to be a rabbit, too small to be a deer. The squat, solid figure took quick steps without disturbing a single leaf, crossed the creek without a splash. A small child was strapped to its back, a head of curly blond hair challenging the sun.

Jessie's feet hit the icy water as she began to run.

Dress Up

From Celia's window, I watched the wolf pad through the snow, weaving between the trees that grew forest-thick behind our house. His thick winter coat could not hide his gaunt frame. The cold made for poor hunting. I thought about putting the pork roast I was defrosting for dinner out on the back stoop, but I knew how stubborn he could be. He would not take it. Turning, I leaned against the windowsill to block the view. Celia sat cross-legged in the center of the room. Her toy palomino pranced in circles around her.

"What do you want to be for Fasching?" I asked.

Celia's large hazel eyes remained fixed on the horse. "I'm too old to dress up," she said.

I gestured at the palomino. "You're not too old. It will be fun. Treats and games, like always."

"Only little kids will be there."

"One last time?"

The palomino stopped mid-step, its right hoof high in the air. Celia furrowed her brow, thinking hard, a look that reminded me of Lowell. "I think I'll be a butterfly."

I could feel a draft at my back. "Are you sure? Wouldn't you rather be a princess?"

Celia picked up the palomino, stroked its blond mane. "I want to be a butterfly."

I folded my arms across my chest. "I don't know if we have a butterfly costume."

"We can use the fairy wings I wore when I was six and the antennas from Lowell's old bee costume." Celia's rosebud lips were tight, her normally pale skin flushed. "It's either a butterfly or I don't go at all."

I sighed and looked behind me. The wolf had disappeared, paw prints in the snow the only trace that he had ever been more than a figment of my imagination. If Celia refused to go, the child in her would be lost. But dressing up in a costume that could take wing might not be any better. "Let's see what we have."

Celia set the palomino back on the floor. It trotted over to its place next to Celia's overflowing toy box, among the dolls, stuffed animals, and board games with half the pieces missing. It planted all four hooves flat on the carpet, flicked the fine hair of its tail, and went still.

CELIA'S BUNNY SLIPPERS SLAPPED against the narrow staircase as she followed me up to the attic. I turned the glass knob of the paneled door, and we entered. Translucent light flooded the space from the small round window at the gable end of the room. The storm window was cracked, the pane crusted with ice. Dust motes danced in the air. A labyrinth of cardboard boxes were piled haphazardly, small boxes placed on large ones, like blocks stacked by a toddler, ready to fall in a heap with the slightest touch. Some were labeled—LPs, Textbooks, Taxes '20-'22," but most were unmarked—Pandora's temptations.

Celia stood near the doorway while I picked through the boxes, carefully lifting them from one precarious pile, stacking them in another just as precarious. The pine board floor creaked beneath my feet. "Where could that box be?" I asked aloud.

"Where it always is. In the far corner, near the window." Celia sounded annoyed.

I shrugged. I was delaying the inevitable. The attic was cold, but Celia wore only shorts and a t-shirt. She always ran hot—my little Yule log. When she was so much smaller, she would fall asleep between Grace and me in our bed, the heat emanating from her keeping away the winter chill.

The box marked "Halloween/Fasching" in Grace's curved script sat exactly where Celia said it was, where we both knew it would be. I brushed away a string of cobwebs. Grace constantly pestered me to sweep them all away, but spiders in a house were good luck.

I opened the box, pulling out bits and pieces of costumes past—skeleton masks, fairy wands, harlequin pants with ruffled cuffs. Celia came closer to watch, putting her hands on a wine crate filled with musty paperbacks. She kicked off her slippers. The bunnies hopped behind an old exercise bike and disappeared. "Sam thinks it's weird, dressing up," she said.

I took out a ballerina's tutu, held it up. It seemed only yesterday Celia was able to fit into it. Now, it was much too small for her. In the past few weeks, I had noticed how her hips had begun to take shape, how her chest had dimpled with the first hint of breasts. "Did you tell Sam that it's like Mardis Gras or Carnival in Rio?"

"I don't think she understands those, either."

I nodded. Sam's parents didn't even let her celebrate Halloween. Sam was a nice girl, though. She and Celia had been friends since first grade. I recalled the first day of school, waiting for the bus with the two of them and Sam's mother, a skeletal woman with thin lips and over sprayed hair. Before Celia hopped on the bus, I gave her a hug and a kiss. She was going out on her own for the first time. I swallowed hard as the bus turned the corner. She would be back in the afternoon, I told myself. I exchanged pleasantries with Sam's mother, but not much more than that. We had been neigh-bors for years, but never connected. It wasn't because she kept giving me that all too familiar look, the one that said, "Why aren't you working, why isn't Grace staying home instead?" No, even in this day and age, that was all too common. The rift between Grace and I started when Lowell was young. She had tried to ban Harry Potter books from the public library. All magic was black magic to people like her. I couldn't help but note that when she put Sam on the bus, her biggest con-cern was that the bow in her daughter's hair wasn't straight.

Halfway into the box, I found bits and pieces from a dozen costumes draped on other, surrounding boxes, and a black cat outfit—white chest, tail stiff, zipper up the back. I held it up for Celia. "You wore this two years ago," I said.

"I'm too big for it now," she said.

I tossed the costume aside, continued rummaging through the box.

"I talk to him sometimes," Celia said.

"Lowell?" When we first entered the attic, I tried to avoid the traces of him. But in speaking his name, I suddenly saw him everywhere—his hockey equipment, his old ten-speed, his baseball card collection stored in Converse shoe boxes.

Celia gestured toward the round window, to the back of the house and the woods. "He's doing okay. Really, he is. He's the one who suggested I be a butterfly," Celia admitted.

"If it's not your decision—"

"He suggested it. I want it," she said.

I returned my attention to the box. The last time I came up here with Lowell, Celia was a toddler, and Lowell was slightly older than Celia was now. We were looking for my old big-bad-wolf mask, the one I wore to win many a New Year's masquerade contest, Grace in tow in her Little Red Riding Hood cloak, basket full of Jell-O shots. Half-drunk women would come and touch the mask, then pull away. "It feels so real," they would say.

At first, I was anxious for Lowell to have the mask. In past months, he had lost interest in what I had to teach him. We fought constantly—about not doing his chores or his homework, about staying out too late with his friends. "You're both too stubborn for your own good," Grace told me. The mask was something we could share. When he first put it on, he could barely breathe through the tiny air holes. Moments later, his howl shook the rafters.

Unlike Lowell, Celia had never lost her interest in my tricks. Prancing horses, slippers that came to life, stepping into landscapes painted with special watercolors. I was hoping with her it would be different. Grace, ever practical, told me this day was inevitable. I wished she was here instead of at work to help me deal with it.

Rummaging on the box's bottom, I found the bee antennae and the pair of fairy wings Celia had mentioned. She snatched the antennae from me, two springs with balls on the ends. She placed them atop her head. They bounced frantically.

The wings were sheer blue and yellow fabric stretched between shaped wire. There was a gap in the wire on one of the wings. The wing was limp, useless.

"Looks like it's busted," I said. I tried not to let my elation creep into my voice. "How about something else?" I held up a princess' tiara.

Celia took the wing from me. She tried to put it back into shape, but it was broken, not bent. Tears welled up in her eyes.

"You're sure this is what you want?"

Celia nodded. I set down the tiara, taking the wing from her. I breathed deep, held it in both hands. I let my fingers run along the wire edges, and as I did, it returned to its original shape. Celia smiled the little girl's smile that comes with a puppy's kiss a new doll at Christmas. She turned her back on me. The wings had safety pins for attaching them to a fairy costume, white tulle that Celia had no need for anymore. My hands shaking, I pinned the wings to the back of her shirt.

Celia spun, arms in the air. "Open the window, Dad."

I shook my head. "It's too cold out."

"Not for me. Open the window, please."

I unlatched the round window. The hinges creaked, frozen from the ice. A blast of frosty air entered the attic. A butterfly, wings blue and gold, fluttered by my ear. It weaved around the snare of a spider's web. I held my breath, hoping it would not ensnare her. The butterfly would not be trapped so easily. She flew in a figure eight around the window's opening. For the briefest of moments, I thought she might not leave. But with a sudden zigzag, she changed direction and left.

Celia wouldn't be gone long, I told myself. She knew better than to stay out in winter. From below, I saw the wolf watching between trees, its hazel eyes furled, familiar, thoughtful.

A pit formed in my stomach. My mind reeled. What had I done? Was it too late? I stretched my hand out the window, holding my finger towards the butterfly as if I could catch her. The butterfly fluttered up into the cloudless sky, towards the cold, bright sun.

Alibi

Gary had just sat down to dinner with his wife, Patty, when the doorbell rang. He got up to answer it, his jacket still on, his tie loose and his top button undone. Two uniformed police officers stood on his stoop. One asked his name. When he gave it, the officer told Gary he was under arrest. He didn't resist. The police officers were surprisingly gentle, one even apologizing for having to handcuff him. It wasn't anything like what he'd seen on TV shows like *Naked City* or *The Detectives*. No doubt, the officers were used to dealing with thugs in t-shirts and leather jackets or weed smoking beatniks, not a mow-the-lawn-on-Saturdays-go-to-church-on-Sundays bookkeeper.

Patty stood in the doorway, hands to her mouth, watched as they escorted him into a waiting patrol car. Neighbors gathered, drawn by the black and white Ford Fairlane's flashing lights, looking on from the opposite curb. From the back seat, Gary couldn't help but notice the crossed arms, the shaking heads, the I'm-not-surprised looks on their faces even though they were no doubt surprised. He stuck his tongue out at them as the car pulled away. He'd have stuck out more than that if not for the handcuffs.

THE OFFICERS SAT GARY DOWN in a room at the station house and left him. It wasn't the Spartan, windowless space with a one-way mirror he expected, but a shared office. Four desks were arranged perpendicular to one another, all but one cluttered with papers, filled ashtrays and stained coffee mugs. A coffee maker next to a small radio sat in the corner. One wall was all windows, shuttered by blinds that blocked out the evening light. On the opposite wall hung a bulletin board tacked with notes, lists, and mugshots of grim men staring straight at the camera. He looked at the faces of those men and wondered if soon he might be one of them.

The wall clock ticked away the minutes, the occasional footsteps could be heard from beyond the shut door. The cuffs were beginning to dig into his wrists. Almost a half hour went by before the doorknob turned and two men walked in, silver badges clipped to their suit jackets.

They introduced themselves as Detectives Raleigh and Joseph. Raleigh seemed young for a detective. He had a full head of perfectly coifed blond hair, a dimpled chin, smokey eyes. His navy suit with a matching checkered tie was well-tailored, and his polished black wingtips clicked when he walked.

Joseph was older, maybe fifty, with a slight paunch. He tried to hide his thinning gray hair with a combover. His plain gold wedding band fit snug on his sausage-like finger. As he sat at the most cluttered desk, he checked the time on his watch he wore military style, face on the inside of his wrist.

Raleigh leaned against the one clean desk directly across from Gary. "You know why you're here?"

"No. Do I need a lawyer?"

"If you want, but we were hoping to clear all this up without that kind of hassle."

Gary shrugged. "Can't really afford one, anyway."

Raleigh twirled a pen between his fingers as he spoke. "That car in your drive, the Galaxie 500. Yours?"

"Yeah."

"Almost new. Must have cost you."

"I get a lot of overtime. April is the busy season."

"Bookkeeper, right? You do taxes."

Gary was surprised at how much Raleigh knew about him but didn't say so. "Among other things."

Raleigh tucked his pen behind his ear. He went to the coffee maker. The coffee had been sitting in it since Gary arrived, giving off a slightly burnt smell. Raleigh poured it into two of the plain, cream-colored mugs that sat beside it and stirred powdered creamer into one. "Tell me, where were you this afternoon?"

"At work, of course," Gary said.

"But you took a long lunch."

"I had an appointment."

Raleigh set the coffee with the creamer in front of Joseph. Joseph hadn't said a word since introducing himself. Instead, he took notes on a yellow legal pad. Raleigh leaned against the desk again, his own mug cradled in both hands.

"What kind of appointment?" Raleigh asked.

"Personal. Look, I'd like to know what this is about."

Joseph paused in his note taking, drank his coffee. A pack of Pall Malls sat amongst the clutter of papers on the desk. He took one out, lit it with a Zippo lighter he produced from his inside breast pocket. He offered one to Raleigh. The other officer waved it away. Instead, he put his pen in his mouth, let it dangle from his lips as he spoke.

"You know East Central Bank?" Raleigh said.

"On Tanning and Coolridge? Sure, not my bank, but I know it."

"Someone robbed it this afternoon."

"You think I robbed a bank?"

"Guy worked alone. Came in with a shot gun. He wore a bandana over his face like it was some kind of Western. Knocked the security guard to the ground and had the tellers empty their tills."

"How much did he get?" Gary asked.

"I thought you could tell me."

"I'm not your guy."

"One of the tellers, she tried to ring the alarm under her counter. Guy fired into the air, scared her so bad she pissed her panties. Had he shot at her instead, he'd be looking at the electric chair. As it is, it's still about twenty years, no parole. We could knock some of that off if you came clean."

"It wasn't me," Gary said.

"No one saw the guy's face 'cause of the bandana. Still, he had your build. He took off in a Galaxie just like yours. The plates match. So, you want to tell me where you really were this afternoon?"

Gary said nothing. Beads of sweat formed on his brow.

"I got to take a leak," Raleigh said to Joseph. He left, taking his coffee with him.

Gary sat in silence with Joseph, watching him take notes. "Why are you still writing?" Gary dared ask.

Joseph put down his pen. He tapped his cigarette into a nearby ash tray, let it to smolder. "I looked you up. Korean War Vet. No record. Mortgage, loan on that car of yours, no other debts. Decent job. So I ask myself, why would this guy rob a bank?"

"I wouldn't." Gary said.

"Look, the FBI will be here soon. Robbing a bank is a federal offense. But we aren't too crazy about the feds around here, hoped to crack this ahead of them. Once they get here though, they won't be as nice as us."

"If you were nice, I wouldn't be in these cuffs."

Joseph got up, went behind Gary, unlocked the handcuffs, tossed them on the otherwise clean desk. Gary rubbed his wrists. "Aren't you afraid I might try to get away?"

Joseph laughed. "I doubt it. You don't look the type."

"I'm not the type that would rob a bank, either, though your partner disagrees."

Joseph returned to his chair. "He's young. Thinks that car of yours is all the evidence we need. Me, I think you were somewhere else this afternoon. What was it? A woman? You don't want your wife to find out? Don't worry, your secret's safe with me."

Gary looked down at his feet. "It was, I mean, it wasn't a woman."

Joseph folded his hands across his chest. "I see. And you think if you give us this guy's name we'll bust him."

"It's what you do."

"It may be a crime, but we've got a robbery on our hands. That's bigger to us than a couple of faggots getting it on in the park."

Gary wanted to tell him it wasn't a park. It was Eric's apartment; fresh sheets, sun coming through the windows, cigarettes and whiskey afterwards. He said nothing. Joseph didn't look like the type who'd appreciate the romance of it all.

"Look, you just give us this guy's name. We ask him if you two had lunch, that's all. He says yes, we move on. What do you say?"

Raleigh returned at that moment, leaving the door open behind him. "You're free to go."

Joseph started to speak, but Raleigh cut him off. "When they went to impound your car, they recorded your plate number. Standard procedure. Found the plates aren't yours. Somebody with the same make and model swapped them out. So it wasn't your car used in the bank robbery after all."

Gary got up slowly, as if unsure they would really let him leave, that this was all game. "I'll need a ride."

Joseph rose. "I'll give you one."

"I'VE MET A LOT OF QUEERS in my line of work," Joseph said. He had just pulled up in front of Gary's house. The porch light was on, but other than that, the house was dark. "Used to work vice. Had to bust up the bars down on Cumberland Avenue, take guys in. Husbands, working stiffs. Guys just like you."

Gary sat in the back seat. He wanted to hop out of the car, hurry into the safety of his own home, but Joseph kept talking.

"You know what? I've changed my mind. I think you did rob that bank, license plates or not. No alibi, so you figured you'd make up this story about being with someone. Make it a guy so you have an excuse not to tell us who it is."

"Why would I do that? I think it'd be worse being in jail for being a homosexual than a bank robber."

Joseph put his arm on the front seat, turned his head so Gary could see his face in the light of the dashboard. "True, but I think you're taking a chance that we wouldn't bust you for it. You're right, by the way. Times are changing. The chief himself told us not to waste our time when we have real criminals to deal with, crime or not. What's another pervert more or less?"

"Lucky me," Gary said. Now that he seemed free and clear, he allowed himself a hint of sarcasm.

"Look, it's none of my business. If you aren't, and you did rob that bank, well, we'll catch up with you eventually. We know where you work, where you live. We'll be watching. And if you are, well, you got a wife in there and it ain't fair to her, living like you do." He nodded to the house.

"That all?"

"Don't drive that car till you get new plates."

Gary got out of the car and walked up the front door. It wasn't until he'd gone inside that Joseph drove away. He almost didn't notice Patty in the dark of the living room, lit only by the porchlight coming through the picture window. She sat on the sofa, legs curled up under her, a vodka tonic in hand. On the coffee table sat Gary's old army duffle, unzipped. Inside, Gary could just make out the packets of crisp ten- and twenty-dollar bills under his license plates.

"You're terrible at hiding things," Patty said. "If they'd have searched the place, they'd have found this in minutes."

"I thought the bottom of the freezer was as good a place as any," Gary replied.

"You mean where you keep those magazines of yours? It was the first place I checked," she replied.

Gary settled into his reading chair, the duffle bag on the coffee table between them. She hadn't found the shotgun in the garage attic, but he wasn't about to mention it.

"So, you going to take this money and run off with that friend of yours?"

"Actually, I was going to give it to you, so you wouldn't have to worry about money when I leave."

She emptied her glass except for the ice. "You think that's what I care about? Money? All I ever wanted was you. I love you."

"I love you, too. Just not like that."

"No, you would rather be with some boy you met in some seedy Cumberland dive." She sucked an ice cube from her glass and crunched it in her teeth.

"I thought I could have both."

"I never should have married you. My sister told me so. 'No, I can change him,' I said. Idiot."

"You going to turn me in?" he asked.

"Now, where would that get me? Names in the papers. Me a laughingstock. You already saw how the neighbors came out to stare."

"Really, I was hoping—"

"You were hoping you could sneak out without having to talk to me. You better go. Your suitcase is on the bed. I found it packed and ready in the closet. Terrible hider."

For the second time that night, he got up out of a chair, wondering if he could really leave. He went to his car in the garage. He had grabbed the plates. but left the money. He told Patty to be careful how she spent it as she poured herself a new drink.

Eric would be waiting for him at his apartment. A new roommate. People might talk, but nothing would be for sure. Confirmed bachelors. A secret life, a dream life.

He shifted into neutral and let the car roll down the drive. He didn't start the engine until he was in the street. He drove carefully, so as not to draw attention. Despite Joseph's warning, the stolen plates were still on it. No time to change them. They would cause new problems if he were pulled over.

The real plates sat on the seat beside him. He had memorized the series of numbers and letters when he first got the car, but now he could not recall them. He looked down at the plates but couldn't make them out in the dashboard light.

Satyr's Dance

It appeared out of the fog, its white tail bright in my head-lights. I swerved, almost running off the road. It turned with me, striking my left bumper. It rolled over the hood and smashed into my sideview mirror before hitting the pavement behind me.

I screeched to a halt, pulled onto the gravel shoulder and got out. My car's engine purred, hazards blinked. I examined the damage: dented bumper, cracked headlight. The sideview mirror hung limp. But unlike everything else that had happened that evening, it was nothing a little money and a couple of days in the shop couldn't fix.

I walked along the road to see if I had killed it, or if it had somehow survived and managed to sprint away. It laid about fifty feet back, straddling the broken yellow line, hooves in the air. I trembled, balled my fists and shoved them in my overcoat pockets to still them. I heard the rumbling of an engine from an approaching vehicle. A white pickup with rusted fenders and a spider web crack in the corner of the windshield pulled up beside me. I recognized it as belonging to Beacon, the handyman who looked after many of the houses along the lake, including ours, keeping an eye on things during the winter months when almost no one was there.

Beacon hopped out of the truck. He had grown a beard since the last time I saw him in August—scraggly and unkempt. His breath mingled with the fog. He looked at me, then down at the body. "That ain't no deer," he said.

"I was about to call the sheriff—" I tried to keep my voice from quivering.

"Don't bother. No signal for another mile. Besides, he'll probably think you're nuts."

Beacon squatted beside the satyr. Stubby horns grew out of a bushy head of hair. It had a pointed goatee and an almost peaceful look on its human face.

"It came out of nowhere," I said, as if feeling the need to explain.

"These things are always in rut this time of year. Makes them go all stupid."

It was only then I noticed the creature's penis still thick between his legs.

"Give me a hand," Beacon said. "There's a place."

I grabbed it by the hooves. Beacon took it by the shoulders and together we lifted it into the back of his pickup. I didn't have to ask if I should come along, and he didn't have to tell me. I went back to my car, shut off the engine and turned off the hazards. Beacon pulled his truck up and I climbed into the passenger seat.

The cab was surprisingly clean. I expected empty Mountain Dew cans and McDonald's wrappers on the floor, maybe the odor of cigarettes, but there was none of that. "Check the glove compartment," Beacon said as he put the truck into gear. Along with the owner's manual and some invoices from a local repair shop I found a pint of Jameson.

"You look like you could use it," Beacon said.

I screwed off the cap and took a swig. It went down smooth. I was surprised at his good taste. He took the bottle from me and took a sip before cradling it between his legs. He drove down the narrow, unpredictable road that curved around the lake with practiced skill. The fog began to lift, replaced by scattered flurries that melted against the windshield. To the left, the lake stretched like blackened ice. To the right, tall trees loomed, the last of their leaves clinging to gnarled branches.

"What are you doing out here, anyway? You're summer people." Beacon said it like it was an insult, which to people like him, who'd lived here all their lives, it probably was. We came on holidays, long weekends, and a few weeks during warmer months. We spent our money in the local restaurants and gift shops. We paid most of the tax burden, but our lives were a three-hour drive away in well-manicured suburbs and city lofts. While people like Beacon were happy to take our money, I was sure that they were just as happy after Labor Day—when we'd leave till next spring, and they'd get their town back.

We turned onto an unmarked road I'd never noticed before. "Where are we headed?"

He drank long and deep. "We have to make a stop first."

We made another turn down a gravel drive hidden by some scraggly yews. The headlights shined onto an unpainted barn, its door broken and its gambrel roof sagging. They stopped in front of a clapboard farmhouse, white paint like lizard scales, yellow lamp light aglow behind sheer curtains.

Beacon got out and was met on the porch by a woman who opened the front door wide. She stood in the threshold, arms folded, while Beacon spoke. He gestured towards me. She responded, obviously angry. I couldn't hear what either of them said with the truck window closed, its engine rumbling, but I could see how she practically spat her words. Beacon spit them back, pointing at her. They stood for a moment, not speaking, then she moved to embrace him. He hugged her back, whispered something in her ear. He kissed her long and deep before heading back to the truck.

"That wasn't your wife," I said as we pulled away. I'd met his wife Grace before. She often came with him on his rounds, helping him by weeding the garden and watering the plants.

"You aren't one to criticize."

I took the bottle he offered and took another swig. It was beginning to have its desired effect. I had stopped shaking, but my head reeled, trying to make sense of what was happening. Deciding I just had to go with it, I kept talking. "How did you know?" I asked.

"I can see it on your face. Besides, why else would you be out here this time of the year if you weren't running from something. She found out, huh? Kicked you out?"

He was focused on the road, couldn't see me shake my head. "Nope. Anna confronted me, and I left. Couldn't face her." I closed my eyes, recalling the pain on her face.

"You'll have to, sooner or later."

"Maybe. You ever feel any guilt? Any regret?

"Sure. Still, can't seem to help myself. Didn't mean for it to happen: falling in love with two women. Can't see a good way out."

"And if you had to make a choice?"

"Hope I never have to."

"Funny thing," I said. "I didn't love her, the other woman. It was pure infatuation. Something to break up the boredom, to remind me, after all this time, that I was still alive. I went into it without caring what would come next, without considering the trouble it would cause. Lust, nothing more."

"That's probably what brought it out." Beacon thumbed towards the back were the satyr lay. "They got a sense for these things."

"You ever hit one?"

"No, but I know what to look for. Besides, for me Wendy's more than just a lay."

We pulled back onto the main road. "Why can't we just leave it in the trees somewhere?"

"Thing deserves more respect. Bring it back to where it belongs. You owe it that. Besides, it has friends."

A pit formed in my stomach. My heart began to race. I thought about the damage those hooves could cause. "Will they blame me? Will I be hurt?"

"We'll have to see," Beacon replied. "But better for you to go to them than them coming to you."

We were both silent for the rest of the drive. As we made our way down blind curves in the dark, I lost track of where we were. We shared the bottle between us until it was gone. By the time Beacon put the truck into park and shut off the engine, I had a pretty good buzz. I fought to walk straight as I got out, tried to appear more sober than I was.

Beacon brought down the tailgate. Together, we took the satyr out. It was rigid, which made it easier to handle. Leaves rustled beneath our feet as we walked, Beacon taking the lead. The ground was rough and uneven, and I stepped wrong more than once, my ankles twisting. The leather soles of my oxfords made it hard to get any traction.

We entered the woods. The satyr felt heavier with each step. I asked Beacon if we could stop for a minute to rest. He shrugged. We set it down and I breathed heavily for a while, wishing I had some water.

"How far?" I asked, feeling a need to whisper.

"We're here," Beacon replied.

Fires sprang up among the trees, like tiki torchlight float-ing mid-air. Flakes of snow twinkled in their light. A bonfire rose not far from us, revealing a clearing of patchy grass and jagged weeds mixed with fallen pine needles. Several satyrs danced around the fire. One played a wood flute. Another one played a lyre. One drank from a horn before passing it along.

They all stopped and turned to face me, Beacon and their dead comrade stiff between us. They all had large erections, which made me uncomfortable. Beacon, for all his seeming confidence, shifted on one leg, as if ready to bolt.

One of them approached us. It was no taller than I was, no taller than the rest. Its brown beard was streaked gray, its face creased. It held the horn of wine in its hand. It stared at the dead satyr, then at Beacon, then at me. It drank, tipping the horn almost upside down. Red wine spilled from its lips, staining its beard. It shoved the horn into my chest so hard I thought it broke a rib. It motioned for me to drink.

I took the horn in both hands, hesitant. It slapped me on the shoulder so hard I almost fell over. The other satyrs gathered around us in a tight semi-circle. I lifted the horn to my lips and took the smallest of sips. The satyr motioned for me to drink deeper. It was oddly sweet and had an aroma like the ashes of a long dead fire. I was about to pass it to Beacon when the satyr snatched the horn away.

The satyrs sang, voices low and guttural, the melody somber and wordless. Beacon took off, leaving me alone with the satyrs. The fires went out and all went dark.

I found myself being lifted. I wanted to resist, but something in me told me not to. The song continued, mixed with the flute and the lyre. I felt hands at my sides, against the back of my neck, at my feet and arms, holding me high, spread eagled, their grips like vices. They set me down gently in a spot tight with the dark trunks of trees. I heard their hoofbeats as they headed away.

A light appeared. Not firelight, more like the glow of the moon, but not the moon, which was eclipsed by the clouds. The light rose from the earth upon a young woman, round in all the right places, with autumn leaves in her chestnut hair. She was draped in a dress that flowed around her, sinking at the shoulders to reveal her right breast. Her face was the shape of a heart unbroken. "They would like you to join us, to make up for the one you killed."

"It was an accident."

"That's no matter. You are one of us. They can see that. They thought I might be able to persuade you to stay."

"Who's us?"

"Those who seek pleasure." She stood in a way that told me I could have her if I wanted. And I did want her. I moved closer. She reached out and took my hand, pulled me close. Her lips neared mine.

"Will this pleasure make me happy?" I asked.

"Has anything ever made you happy?" She smiled. A smile intended to hold onto me, to never let me go. There was something in that smile, though. The corners of her lips too pointed. Her teeth too white. Her slender eyebrows arched, and her dark eyes widened. I turned my head, as if staring too deep would mean falling into an abyss.

I pulled away, ran in the direction I thought I had come. The satyrs appeared between the trees. They no longer sang. I tripped over either a rock or a tree root, it was hard to tell. I scrambled up, kept running. I heard footsteps. I dropped to the ground, buried my head, remained still, holding my breath, hoping they'd miss me in the dark.

Hands lifted me by the shoulders. It was Beacon. Without a word, he led me out of the trees back to his truck. We got in and he started it up.

"Wish we had more whiskey." I rubbed my hands together. They were cold, dead as ice.

"Seems you had enough."

"What did you see out there?"

"Nothing. I never saw anything. Never have. Never will. You?"

"I don't know."

By the time we reached my car, I had sobered up enough to drive if I took it slow, even though my head was still fuzzy.

I took my wallet out and handed what cash I had to Beacon. He shoved it into his breast pocket.

"You should go home. Try to make things right." Beacon said. "You're summer people."

I nodded. I thought about Anna, waiting at home, no doubt worried sick despite my mistakes. I had a lot to atone for, and if I was lucky, she'd give me a chance.

Beacon waited as I got out and went back to my car, with its dangling side mirror and dented bumper. I put my hand over the hood. The engine was strangely still warm. I rubbed my palms over it until the life came back.

Standing Still

"Let's play Statue Maker." Hannah stood, turning down the music on the turntable as she made the suggestion, which, if you knew her, was not a suggestion at all.

We were in her living room, all of us drunk and some of us more than a little stoned. The album playing was one she had found in a second-hand store, full of skips and scratches with a heavy bass and a funk guitar played on the turntable. The idle chatter which had started our little party to celebrate the survival of another semester had dwindled as evening became night and night turned to early morning.

"What's Statue Maker?" Sonja asked. She was sitting on Jay's lap, absent-mindedly playing with the brown curls at his nape. Her nails were long and painted dark.

Hannah explained, "One of us is the statue maker. Another is the buyer. The rest of you are statues." She gestured to the room. Along with Sonja, Jay, and myself, there was Derek, who was sitting in the overstuffed chair, his eyes narrow slits, like he was on the verge of passing out. You had to know him to realize that was how he always looked, as if he was in a permanent haze.

"The statue maker spins the rest of you around one-by-one and lets go. However you land, you have to stay that way, like a statue."

"Stoned still," Derek said. We all laughed.

"The statue maker takes the buyer around. He stops at each of you and the statue maker decides what you are based on how you landed. You have to act out whatever it is you are supposed to be—mummy, eagle, ballerina, whatever. In the end, the buyer decides which one to buy."

"Then what?" Sonja asked.

"You win," Hannah says.

"I mean, what happens to the statue once you buy it?" She smiled at Jay.

"It was never part of the game," Hannah replied. "We were kids."

"That's not how I remember it," Derek said. "In our version, you just stood still, and the first one to move lost."

"Boring," Jay replied.

"My apartment, my rules," Hannah said.

"It's Sonja's apartment, too."

"I'm just a roommate," Sonja deferred. "Hannah's on the lease." She said this like this was some sort of mock trial, as if she was making a point of law.

I didn't want to play. I was happy to sit and nurse what should have been my last beer and become lost in the lingering scent of pot mixed with the sandalwood incense Hannah liked so much. Maybe just fall asleep here, have Hannah take off my shoes, throw a blanket over me while I snored. Dream, perhaps of Hannah, but most likely of Sonja. Dreams I would not remember when I woke. Head aching, my mouth full of cotton, and a pang in my stomach that seemed like it would never go away.

Jay pulled Sonja toward him. He had his hand up her shirt. "I wouldn't mind being statue maker. I like the idea of this one having to do whatever I say."

Sonja looked down, embarrassed. She tried to move his hand away, but it wouldn't budge.

Hannah shook her head. "Come on."

We all filed out of the apartment. I made sure Hannah and I were the last to leave. "He's a pig," I said, referring to Jay. "She looks up to you. Can't you do something?"

Hannah pressed against me. She was almost my height. Our hips, what there was of them, touched. We were both tall and bony, which might have been part of the initial attraction.

"Why don't *you* do something?" she asked.

"Jay's my friend," I replied.

"That's just an excuse."

"I could use your help."

We headed down the stairs. Hannah sighed, "I guess I owe you for how I used to treat you. For not being a very good girlfriend."

"You weren't that bad."

"Thanks." Sarcasm dripped from her pale lips. "We weren't a good fit for each other. We both know it. I'm too controlling and you're too easy to control."

I didn't respond. I recalled the day we broke up. The night was steamy, the windows open to the still air. Us both naked, side-by-side, sweating against a thin sheet draped over us. She was the one who said the words, told me it was over. I merely agreed.

HANNAH AND SONJA LIVED in a century-old apartment building, three stories, U-shaped with a courtyard in the center. The open end was fenced with wrought iron. The center of the gate adorned with the face of a lion. Gargoyles perched on the roof overhead. A cat stalked across one of the wide stone window ledges. There was a flood light above the main door, and a few of the apartments above had a light on or two. Other than that, everything was dark. Summer was a month away, but still, the air was warm.

"Are we still going to play?" I said. "I don't want to wake anyone up."

"No one's gonna care," Derek replied. It was a neighborhood of students and transients. People lived here for only a short while before they graduated or saved some money or got a new job and could afford to move to someplace better. Beyond the courtyard, cars raced up and down the main drag. The whir of sirens and the blare of car alarms weren't uncommon.

"Statues don't make noise," Hannah replied. "I'll be the statue maker."

"Why *you*?" Jay asked. Hannah gave him a sideways look, hard and sharp. It was a look she often gave me when we were dating. We reunited a couple of months before at a St. Patrick's Day party. It was the first time we'd seen each other since our breakup. We sat outside on a park bench and had a long talk. In the end, we agreed we'd always be friends. We kissed to seal the deal, but there was no passion in it.

"Sonja, you're the buyer." Hannah took her arm, pulled her away from Jay. Jay started to protest. We had been dormmates freshman year. Not that he was in the room much. He was always with some girl or another. Still was. He never cared for Hannah, especially when we were dating. He hit on her once. She saw right through his crap. He still came around though, because Hannah always had pot, and of course, because Sonja was there.

"It's okay," Sonja said. "I'd barf if you spun me around."

So, it was decided. While Sonja sat on the front stoop, Hannah spun each of the guys around in turn. She used our drunkenness to her advantage. She clasped our hands in hers and turned us each three times before letting go. Derek stumbled as he came to a stop, but remained on his feet, his back to her. Jay tried to stay on his feet as he came to a stop but stumbled and landed on his stomach. Sonja laughed.

When my turn came, Hannah gripped me by the wrists and spun me so fast I thought my arms would rip from my shoulders. She spun me an extra time, grinning widely, her long dark hair falling across her face. Bile rose up in my throat. She let go and I tripped as I left her clasp. I ended up on one knee, the palms of my hands sank deep into the grass.

"Now, no one move," Hannah said. I was facing away from her but could hear her, that voice she used when she absolutely wanted her way.

I could just make out Derek to my far right. Jay closer to me on my left. None of us moved. I tried to lift one of my hands from the ground, ever so slightly, but found that I couldn't.

Hannah spoke like a ringmaster announcing an act, "Welcome to Hannah's House of Magnificent Statues. What can I get for you?"

"I don't know," Sonja said, playing along, "What do you have?"

Hannah took Sonja by the hand, walked her over to Derek. She considered him a moment. "Here is a very special piece. We call it the Zombie." She pressed an imaginary button on Derek's back. He started moving in a wide circle, his arms limp, his knees locked. He made moaning sounds. As he turned towards me, I could see the blank look in his eyes. He partly opened his mouth. His naturally dark skin appeared ashen in the glow of the security light.

I smelled something similar to rotten flesh. He finished his circle while Sonja considered him, Hannah standing with her arms crossed. She reached out, hit the imaginary button. Derek became a statue again.

"Scary," she said. "He'd be a big hit at my next Halloween party, but I don't know if I'd want him around full time."

"Fair enough." Hannah escorted her to where Jay lay on the ground.

"This one can be quite dangerous," Hannah said.

"Seems harmless enough. Kind of cute. What do you call him?"

"Lucifer's Tail." Hannah pressed her heel hard into Jay's back. If it hurt, he didn't show it. He started to squirm though, sliding through the grass, contorting himself in ways I didn't think possible for a human being. He coiled his body, his arms tight against him as if they didn't exist. It appeared as if he was struggling to resist, his neck muscles tight, his eyes wide, but he couldn't break free. He rose and faced the two women. He opened his mouth and hissed. His tongue went in and out. I wasn't sure but could have sworn it was forked.

He lunged at Sonja, his jaws wide, as I'd seen him do so often with her when he wanted a wet, sloppy kiss. Normally, she'd oblige, but this time she stepped back, clung to Hannah's arm. Hannah hissed back. Jay recoiled, and as he did, Hannah reached out and hit him on the back again. He stopped, his body still wrapped around itself.

"I don't want to play anymore," Sonja said, her voice quivering. She was shaking. I wanted to get up, call this all off, go to her, take her home, but I couldn't move.

"You shouldn't have made him like that."

"He's the way he is," Hannah said. Sonja opened her mouth to speak again, but Hannah hushed her with a finger to her lips. She held her friend for a few moments, whispered something into her ear. Afterwards, Sonja calmed down. She stopped shaking, but her eyes were still wide as Hannah led her to me. She pressed an imaginary button at my temple. I imagined, if she wanted, she could press it all the way into my brain. She did not name me, so I did not move.

"What is it?" asked Sonja. "What does it do?"

"Absolutely nothing. It's just a statue, nothing more."

By now, I had enough of Hannah's game. I tried to rise but found I couldn't. I couldn't move my hands or feet, any part of me. I tried to call out, but without being able to open my mouth, all that came out was a loud grunt.

Sonja frowned. That frown hurt more than anything Hannah could have done to me. "Not very impressive."

Hannah tilted her head. "No. No, he's not. So, which will it be—zombie man, snake boy, or the rock here?"

Sonja walked back over to Jay. "He may be a slithering reptile, but he's my slithering reptile." She went to push the imaginary button on Jay's back. A wry smile appeared on his face. I thought I could still see sharpened teeth.

I willed myself to move again, just a little. I focused on my little finger. Perhaps, if I concentrated all my energy to that one spot, something would happen. I pictured Sonja going home with him. Jay wrapping himself around her, his tongue still forked. I allowed the image to provide me focus. My little finger trembled slightly.

Jay straightened, moving again. Sonja wrapped her arms around him, kissed him. Hannah looked at them, then at me, eyebrows arched to sharpened points.

I raised my finger from the ground, slowly but surely. The rest of my fingers, then my hand, followed. I lifted my arm like some sort of 50s sci-fi robot.

Derek had been released from his zombie state. For him, the game was over. "It's alive!" he shouted.

Sonja and Jay were heading back inside. I rose to my feet. My joints creaked as I moved towards them, but I was taking long strides, and they were swaying as they walked. I reached the door at the same time as them.

Jay turned to me and as he did, I hit him in the jaw. My punch was harder than I had thought possible. I heard the cracking of bone.

Jay lay on the ground, stunned. He was wiggling his jaw in his hand. It wasn't broken but should have been. Sonja knelt beside him, her arm around his shoulder. She glared at me.

A couple of lights came on in the windows above. A few heads peaked out. Someone called out that they were trying to sleep. Suddenly sober, I turned away, started out of the courtyard, my gait stiff. Sonja would never see me the way she saw Jay. He would never change, even if I crushed every bone in his body. But I had to find this out for myself. Had to do it myself. Hannah knew me. Knew *this*.

Derek watched me go. Hannah stood on the sidewalk, leaning against the wrought iron fence. In the confusion, I didn't realize she'd gotten ahead of me.

"I told you I'd take care of things," she said.

I hurried past her, each step smoother than the next. I clenched and unclenched my fist. It would hurt for at least a week. Hannah remained there, waiting as if expecting me to thank her.

I wasn't sure if I should.

It Happened on Jackson Street

Sparky and Tinsel had a hard time finding a place to get a drink on Christmas Eve. It was already past dinnertime when they got done with their last shift as Santa's elves at Gurney's Holiday Village. They left the department store through the employee exit on Jackson Street to empty sidewalks and closed shops. A few errant cars, some cabs and the occasional bus the only vehicles on the normally bumper to bumper boulevard.

They walked close together, hands in their pockets, chins down to guard against the wind, streetlamps a bright white, traffic signals blinking. Despite the cold, it hadn't snowed—no white Christmas this year.

After several blocks, the downtown high rises abruptly gave way to a neighborhood of three flats and bungalows. There they found a corner bar with neon Pabst and Miller Lite signs in the windows and "Winnie's Place" stenciled on the door.

The bar was narrow and dimly lit. Red and green lights draped the paneled walls in a futile attempt to make the place look more festive. Only a few barstools were taken. All but one table was free. No one was using the dart board or the pool table. More people than not had someplace better to be on this silent night.

A TV over the bar aired *It's a Wonderful Life* with the sound off, Donna Reed silently singing "Buffalo Gals." Christmas music piped in from some unknown source, "Winter Wonderland" sung by Louis Armstrong in his unmistakable, gravelly voice.

They chose a table in the corner. The bartender, an older woman, more wrinkles than skin, was the only one working. She came out from behind the bar to take their order. Tinsel asked if she was *the* Winnie. The bartender told her proudly that she was. "Twenty years and counting," she said. "My kids all moved away, so I figured why not be open for anyone with nowhere else to go."

Sparky ordered a beer, whatever they had that was dark and wintery. Tinsel ordered the same. Sparky was surprised at this. He took her for the kind of person who preferred a white wine spritzer or some mixed drink sweet with fruit juice. Winnie hurried behind the bar to pull the drafts from the tap.

No one paid any attention to the two elves. Not that they looked like elves anymore. They turned in their pointed shoes and belled hats when they received their last paychecks. Their slight frames were hidden beneath bulky sweaters and wool coats.

"You still going home for Christmas?" Sparky asked Tinsel. It wasn't her real name, no more than Sparky was his. Elf names were given to them in training, several weeks before, when Gurney's was replacing pumpkin and ghost displays with lighted trees and wreaths. Still, the name Tinsel fit her well. Her hair was dyed a silver that shimmered even in the bar's dim light. When they met that first day of orientation, he asked if she had done it for the season. She just smiled, and that smile made his heart skip a beat.

"My mom wants me home. Pretty traditional. Gifts under the tree, a ham in the oven. Nieces and nephews ripping open their presents. I take the last train to the burbs tonight. You?"

Winnie brought their beers. Sparky drank. The two elves hit it off from that first day of orientation. They were both in school trying to make some extra holiday money. They had the same sense of humor and would spend breaks in the department store lunchroom making fun of the impatient fathers and demanding mothers, all waiting in line so their children could ask Santa for toys that would be forgotten in a week, or worse yet, break into tears at having been forced onto an old man's lap. Still, this was the first time they'd talked about their lives outside of work. Sparky was weary of how much to tell Tinsel, self-conscious of what she might think of him. "Get some sleep, I guess," he said.

"You don't have anyone?"

"My mom died young."

"And your dad?"

"He lives in one of those big houses on Hampton Hill. He has a new wife and a couple of young kids. A new family. We never got along that well anyway. He's infinitely practical. The last time we got together, we had a big fight. He thinks it's a waste, me trying to be an actor. Thinks I should be an accountant or an engineer. 'You're too smart to waste your life,' he told me. Refused to pay for my school even though he can afford it. Can't think of what he'd say if he knew I'd been working as a Santa's elf."

"It's a noble profession," Tinsel replied.

"It paid better than being a store clerk at Christmas," he said.

Tinsel frowned and sipped her beer. Sparky half-hoped she might ask him to come home with her. Thinking about it, though, he'd say no thanks. He'd like to spend more time with her, but a holiday in a house full of strangers would make him feel awkward, and he didn't want her pity.

Winnie appeared with a bowl of pretzels. "Merry Christmas," she said with a wink.

"She thinks we're a couple," Tinsel said after she'd gone.

Sparky wished it were true. When they were working, Tinsel would sometimes run her hand across his back as she passed. At first, he thought this meant something, but as he watched her with the other elves, he saw her do this with them as well, realized it's just how she was.

The front door of the bar slammed open, and a Santa stumbled in. It wasn't one of the rosy cheeked men who worked the lines at Gurney's, who saw playing Santa as a calling akin to tending lepers in India or feeding starving African children. Their suits were always neatly pressed, their boots and belts polished to a shine, beards full and white. This Santa looked like he hadn't had a good meal in days, his tattered red coat too big on him. His beard was a scraggly, dripping gray, his face sunken and sallow.

He was obviously drunk. He staggered to the bar, ordered a shot. Winnie served him hesitantly. He downed the drink and tried to make conversation with the man sitting on the stool next to him, a guy in a heavy flannel who ignored him, eyes fixed on the TV, George Bailey standing on the bridge contemplating jumping into the icy water below.

The Santa looked around the bar, spotted Tinsel and Sparky in the corner. He headed to them, sat down at their table without waiting for an invitation.

"I know what you want," he said, leaning in close to Sparky. His breath smelled of peppermint, as if he'd just finished a bottle of schnapps.

"Santa can always tell." He put a finger to his nose.

"Leave those two kids alone," Winnie said from the bar.

"We're just talking," he slurred.

She folded her arms. "You need to go. Christmas or not."

He tried to wave her away with a once white glove, but she stood her ground. Slowly, he got up and left the bar.

"Sorry about that," Winnie said as she dropped off two more beers on the house and went to wait on three young men who had just entered and taken a table by the windows.

"Some people don't deserve to wear the suit," Tinsel said.

Sparky watched him go out the door. "Kind of feel sorry for him. There but for the grace of God, you know. I worry if one day that might be me."

"It doesn't have to be. You have family."

He finished his first beer, started on the next one. Tinsel had hardly touched hers. "It's not that easy," he said.

Tinsel stared hard at him. Her eyes, usually soft and blue, appeared as a hard gray. "Liar. He's still your dad. I bet he misses you, too." She took out her phone, began typing.

"What are you doing?" Sparky asked.

"Showing you how easy it is," Tinsel replied. "Your ride will be here in a few minutes."

"I can walk to my apartment."

"You're not going to your apartment," Tinsel said.

Sparky opened his mouth to protest but stopped himself. He looked around the bar at the other people with nowhere better to be. "It'll be awkward. We've said a lot of things that are hard to take back."

"You'll manage."

They left their beers on the table. Sparky paid. Tinsel left a healthy tip. They wished Winnie happy holidays. She was talking to the man in flannel at the bar but managed a wave and a smile. On TV, George Bailey was silently learning what the world would be like without him while Bing Crosby crooned "I'll be Home for Christmas."

The wind had died, and the night was clear. There was no moon, only stars. After a few moments, a sedan with an Uber sticker pulled up. Tinsel opened the door. As Sparky got inside, she gave him a peck on the cheek. A friendly kiss, nothing more. Still, it was more than Sparky had hoped for.

Tinsel listened as Sparky gave the driver an address on Hampton Hill. They bade each other Merry Christmas and she shut the door, watched the sedan make a left turn and disappear.

"So, were you able to give him what he wanted?"

Tinsel turned to see the drunken Santa standing near the curb. He stood upright, his voice no longer slurred. His eyes twinkled in the lamplight. The scent of peppermint remained.

"No, not what he wanted. What he wanted was me. What he needed, though? He got that, or at least, I think he will."

The Santa came up to her, put a hand on her shoulder. "Have some time before your train? There are still more people to help."

"There's always time," Tinsel said.

The man in flannel slammed open the bar door. He looked the Santa up and down. "Ho! Ho! Ho!" he said, his voice sarcastic. There was a sadness in his eyes. He started away, a stagger in his step.

The Santa and Tinsel exchanged a glance and hurried to sidle up on either side of him, took him by each arm, steadied him as he walked.

The Correct Response

Okinaw, Wisconsin was no Haiti or Jamaica, or even New Orleans. Ten miles off Route 29, it was just a little town with one main street, a diner, two churches, three bars, a grocery, and a gas station. No tradition of voodoo. No witchdoctors. No animal sacrifices to spirits of the dead. It was a far cry from home.

I drove in on a hazy Sunday afternoon in August. The parking lot of the First Methodist Church was already empty. The parking lot of Dino's Bar was already full. I headed for the bar. I needed directions. All I had was the return address on the letter Mrs. Terrence had sent me, and on these rural roads, with all their As and KKs, I'd be lost in no time. GPS could only get me so far in the boondocks. There was always someone in a bar willing to help.

The place was darker than it should have been for a day so bright. Everyone was white, mostly male, wearing CAT and John Deere trucker caps, smoking cigarettes and drinking beer, talking in low tones while the Green Bay Packers played on the TV above the bar. A few of them glanced my way when I entered, but no one paid much attention. I had to remind myself that after my long drive, I was no longer in the Deep South but the Upper Midwest. I was probably the first black man they had seen in months.

I found an empty stool at the end of the bar. The bartender, a middle-aged dishwater blond, smiled at me from across the way as she served an old man a shot of something dark. It was an awkward smile, as if she knew who and what I was. Some people had that gift, witches mainly, raised in the art, but way up here? As she came my way and asked me what I wanted, I shrugged off the thought. Her smile was just a response to a stranger, I decided.

"I'll have whatever's on tap," I said. She pulled out a glass. She had probably been pretty when she was younger, maybe homecoming queen or milk queen, or whatever they called it around here. Over time, her looks had faded. Lines had formed around her eyes like dry canals, her lips had thinned, her skin had paled.

The man sitting on the stool next to mine glanced sideways at me. He had a pot belly and wore a sleeveless t-shirt that revealed thick arms and a cobra tattoo on his left shoulder. "Who's winning?" I asked, nodding at the TV. The bartender served me my beer.

"Packers," he answered, "Not that it matters in preseason."

"Yeah," I replied. I didn't follow football. It was too emotional a sport. I only asked about it because I'd learned that it helps to make a connection with people, to take an interest in their interests.

He sized me up. "You look big enough. You ever play?" he asked.

"No," I said. I drank my beer, wishing I could taste it. It seemed like a waste. I don't need to drink, but I would have looked conspicuous otherwise.

"Too bad. I used to play in high school. All-State, linebacker on defense, running back on offense. Could've gone to college. Got lots of offers."

"What happened?" It was polite to ask. People always wanted to talk to me, tell me things they wouldn't tell anyone else. As if they sensed that I would not, could not, judge them.

He shrugged. "No motivation, I guess. Too much work."

I finished my beer, and he bought me another even though I hadn't asked for it. The score flashed on the screen: Packers 28, Tampa Bay 9.

"You just passing through?" he asked.

"I'm looking for the Terrence Farm. Any idea where that is?"

The man frowned. "Sorry, can't help you."

A wiry guy with sideburns and a dirty t-shirt approached from somewhere in the back. The man with the tattoo slapped him on the chest and got up. They whispered to each other as they walked away. Before leaving the bar, Sideburns glanced back at me.

"Don't mind them," the bartender said. "Lot of people like that, since Jerry Terrence's accident. Not every day someone comes back to life. They're just superstitious. They don't buy the doctor's explanation about Jerry having been in a deep coma. They think Jerry's the walking dead."

"Not you, though?" I asked.

She shrugged. "I just feel bad for his mom."

"Can you tell me where their house is?" I asked. "I may be able to help."

She pulled out a pen and scribbled a map on a napkin. "It's only about five miles," she said, "and here's my number, in case you get lost, or maybe for later, if you need a place to stay. No hotels around here." She smiled again, less awkward this time, and held out her hand. "My name's Denise."

"Ben," I replied, taking it. "You married?"

"Divorced," she answered.

Folding the napkin into my shirt pocket, I left her a hefty tip and walked out. In the parking lot, Tattoo and Sideburns waited for me. They leaned on the hood of my car, conspicuous with its Louisiana plates. Tattoo stood with his arms folded. Sideburns twirled a thick-bladed hunting knife in his hand.

"We've had enough crap here since Jerry died," Tattoo said. "The cops, TV, social media. We don't want anymore."

"I don't want trouble," I replied.

"Well, if you don't want trouble, you had better leave and not come back," he said. He pressed the blade of his knife lightly across his fingertips as if to test its sharpness.

"You don't want to mess with me," I said.

"Why not?" Tattoo stepped forward.

Fixing my eyes on him, I reached into my pocket, pulled out a Zippo lighter, turned the flame up as high as it could go. I flicked it. The flame shot up several inches. I placed my hand over that flame, not so close as to snuff it out, but close enough for it to hurt if I had been anyone else.

I felt the heat, but there was no pain. The two men watched as I kept my hand in place for ten seconds, thirty seconds, a full minute. I kept looking straight at them, unflinching, my face locked in a grim expression that revealed nothing. They refused to meet my gaze. They glanced at each other, then slowly backed away.

"I can keep this up for hours, days even, if I want," I said. "So, you can cut me all you want. You can beat me to a pulp. I've been through it all before. It won't make any difference. I'm not leaving until I'm ready."

I shut off the lighter, put it back in my pocket. They didn't try to stop me as I got into my car.

MRS. TERRENCE WAS A SWEET WOMAN, short and round with curly white hair. She welcomed me into her house as if I was a long-lost cousin. "I had Jerry late in life," she explained as we drank iced tea in her kitchen. All the windows in the little farmhouse were open. An old fan beat rhythmically in the corner. "Since my husband Joe passed on, Jerry's all I've had. He had always taken care of the place."

I sipped my tea and listened silently, even though she had said all this in the letter she had sent me, the letter that brought me here. It would have been impolite not to listen. Earlier, heading up the drive, I noticed that the house had a new coat of paint, the barn had a lot of its siding replaced, and someone had begun reshingling the roof.

"He works harder now than ever, but he's not my Jerry. He doesn't have Jerry's laugh, his touch, his warmth. He just works and, at the end of the day, goes to his room. He watches TV, whatever's on, or sits in the dark, staring out the window. He eats only when I make him. I haven't gotten a hug or an 'I love you' since the accident. Jesus, what have I done?"

"Where did you get the knowledge?" I asked.

"My grandmother, she was from Mississippi. A big old estate with lots of hired hands, coloreds, like yourself. There was an old cook there, she taught my grandmother things, and my grandmother taught them to me."

"You remembered, after all these years?" I asked. I let the coloreds comment pass. This woman was from a different time, a different place. In a way, so was I. Besides, I was here to help her, help Jerry, if I could. That's why I answered her letter. Anyway, I'm impossible to offend.

"My grandmother had a journal. The whole ritual was there, the ingredients, the incantations. It was easy, once I read it. Like following a recipe."

"Is that how you knew about me as well?"

She nodded.

"Where's the journal now?" I asked.

"I burned it, so it couldn't be used again. I felt so guilty, I knew it was wrong, but I had already buried my husband, I couldn't stand to lose my son as well. And now it seems I've lost him anyway."

She broke down, sobbing heavily in her hands. Rising from my chair, I walked around her and put a hand on her shoulder. "Everything will be all right, Mrs. Terrence," I said, a rehearsed softness in my voice.

Jerry entered then, letting the flimsy screen door slam shut behind him. He was in his early twenties, lanky with tousled dark hair. He took no notice of me, a strange man in the middle of his kitchen, or of his mother, crying at the table. He went to the sink, walking slowly and deliberately, poured himself a glass of water, drank it down. A habit, I guessed, left over from before. I knew he didn't need it. Still, it was a good sign, to have something left of your former life.

He would have walked right out again, but I stepped in front of him, held out my hand.

"Hi, Jerry," I said. "My name's Ben."

He didn't answer, didn't shake my hand. I noticed the scar on his forehead, how pale his skin was. The traces of mortician's make-up.

"I've come a long way," I said. Our eyes met, and for a moment, I thought I had made a connection. But he was looking through me, not at me. He brushed my shoulder as he headed back outside. The screen door didn't close all the way, lingered halfway between open and shut in the still air.

Mrs. Terrence's crying finally subsided. "Can you do any-thing?" she asked.

Jerry and I had met, and it didn't go well. Still, it didn't go badly, either. Sometimes they got violent. Violence that came from anger—at death, at whoever brought them back, at me for reminding them what they were, was the only emotion some of them had left. In those cases, my job was twice as hard. Still, I didn't want to push anything. "Not today," I said. Then, reading the despair on her face quickly added, "but I'm sure I can, eventually."

She appeared pleased at that. It was the right thing to say, even if it was a lie. This could go either way. Either I would get through to Jerry, or he would have to be destroyed.

AS I DROVE BACK INTO TOWN, I thought about the napkin with Denise's number in my pocket and decided to give her a call. To pass the time, I told myself, a half-truth. She reminded me of someone, a face vaguely recalled from the distant past. Memories of those days were rare. They had to be nurtured or they would be lost.

Denise lived in a small, run-down house near the tracks on the edge of town. That night, I went through the motions, feigning the passion, the eroticism, the strength which she so obviously craved. I had become so good at it over years of practice that she didn't even notice that it was all an act. Afterwards, we lay on our backs in her bed. Outside, a freight train passed.

"Sorry," she said. "Sometimes it feels like they're running through the room. We've done enough bed-shaking tonight." She laughed and I laughed with her.

"It's okay," I said.

"It was great," she replied. "I mean greater than great, better than ever."

"You don't have to flatter me," I said. "I don't have much of an ego."

She was silent for a moment. I had said the wrong thing. Even after all this time, I was no good at accepting compliments.

"How's Jerry?" she asked after a while. "Can you help him?"

"Maybe," I replied, realizing that Denise wasn't as squeamish as most on the subject, that I could talk to her more matter-of-factly. "Some you can, some you can't. In some, there's still a spark, a knowledge of what it's like to be alive, the core of their former selves. Sometimes, that core is fear, hate, anger. Sometimes, it's love, joy, compassion. For others, nothing is left. They're just a shell." I thought about the syringe tucked away in my bag.

"Which is Jerry?" she asked.

"I don't know yet. That's why I'm here."

I rolled onto my side. She sidled up close. With her fingertip, she traced the scars that lined my back like dried riverbeds. I could feel its pressure but couldn't sense its tenderness.

"Where'd you get these?" she asked.

"Run in with a bunch of guys, didn't like the color of my skin. It was a long time ago." The memories again, of the woman, so much like Denise, the blond, white woman whose love had cost me my life. The love who had once meant the world to me, but whose name I could no longer recall.

Denise kissed my back. "Well, I like your skin. I like your scars. They give you character. Do they hurt?"

"Nothing hurts anymore," I replied.

MRS. TERRENCE HAD TOLD ME that Jerry spent mornings in the fields, and I wouldn't be able to see him until later in the day. Denise had to work. Dino's opened at nine a.m. "Yes," Dense said, "There are always people waiting at the door for their first drink of the day." With nothing better to do, I decided to walk down Main Street. Killing time.

Weeds poked through cracked sidewalks. A few cars drove slowly past, most ignoring the stoplight at the intersection. Half the store fronts were empty, faded lettering on their doors hinting at the town which once had been—First National Bank, Lang Brothers Realty, Holmes Fine Furnishings. The shops that were still open—the barbershop, the laundry, and of course, the bars—had their doors propped open to welcome the summer heat. A few customers came and went, none of them paying me any attention. There were none of the polite hellos you usually got in a town this size. By now, most likely, word had gotten around about me.

Walking past the movie theater, I read its marquee, half the letters dangling. It advertised one show a night with a matinee on Saturday. Next to the theater was Rita's Diner. I peeked in its pane glass window. It was empty except for two old men, sitting at a table, playing cards—gin rummy, I believed—and drinking coffee. They moved lazily, putting the cards down as if in slow motion. A waitress came by with a coffee pot and refilled their cups. None of them spoke. There was no hurry. Killing time.

LATE THAT AFTERNOON, I found Jerry in his room, sitting on the edge of his bed, staring out the window. "Hot day," I said, attempting small talk. Jerry didn't respond. His eyes were fixed on a point far out in the field. I sat down next to him. "Do you know why I'm here, Jerry?"

Still no answer.

"Your mother sent for me. She loves you very much. Do you know what love is, Jerry?"

Jerry didn't even blink.

"I'm here to tell you you're not alone, Jerry. There are lots of people like you, like me. You don't have to live like this." I got up and moved around to face him, blocking his view of the outside world. "You have to meet me part way, though, Jerry. You have to help yourself."

His gaze was stoic, impenetrable, as if he took it all in but saw nothing. I'd get no more from him that day. I walked out, debating whether or not to shut the door, then deciding in the end that, at least to Jerry, it didn't really matter.

AFTER A DINNER OF BURRITOS and refried beans, I helped Denise with the dishes the way a good guest should. She had gone to all the trouble of preparing the meal. I thought it best not to tell her I didn't need to eat. As she washed and I dried, she asked me how Jerry was doing.

"Not well," I said. "He's completely unresponsive."

"No spark?" she asked.

"No spark."

"So, what's next?"

"One more session," I said. "To try to get through to him. There are a couple of tricks I can use. Otherwise..."

"Otherwise, what?"

I had filled the syringe that evening, just in case. "Let's just say Jerry would be better off not being around at all."

Denise dropped the plate she was washing into the sudsy water. She looked at me, shocked, angered. "How could you? I mean, his poor mother?"

"You have to understand what it's like. If he remains this way, he doesn't care. And as for his mother, she'll just be back where she started from. She'll bury him. She'll mourn. Like she should have in the first place."

"It's so cruel," she said, drying her hands on a towel. There were still some dirty dishes left.

"People have no idea how to deal with death. Our rituals are completely inadequate. That's why there are people like Jerry. That's the cruelty. Creating emotional eunuchs because we're too selfish to let a loved one go."

"But shouldn't he have more time?"

"I know quick how it will be," I answered.

She walked into the bedroom. I finished up the dishes. Later, despite everything, we made love again. It was hard for me to tell who was more distant.

JERRY AND I WERE BACK IN HIS ROOM, sitting side-by-side on his bed. I was asking Jerry questions, talking to him in soothing tones, as if trying to talk a suicide down from a ledge. I asked him about his mother, any pets he may have had, friends and girlfriends, anything to get a response. I got nothing, not a word, not a look, not even a nod. My hand was folded over the syringe.

"I know you're in there, Jerry. I know what it's like. You want to come out. You want to shout at the world. Shout, Jerry, shout!" My voice was almost at a fevered pitch, *my* spark, *my* life, showing through. Still, he didn't respond. I raised the syringe slightly, aiming it at his arm. Decapitations were traditional, but messy. This was quick and clean. He took no notice of even that, a threat to his existence. I held back, though. I had one last card to play.

"Tell me about your death, Jerry," I said. I raised the syringe a little higher, even with his shoulder, prepared to use it. But then, suddenly, he turned to me, blinking twice. He frowned. His eyes looked sad, lost.

I lowered the syringe, got up, and left. For now, it was enough.

I WENT BACK TO DENISE'S. She made us spaghetti with home-made sauce. I complimented her on it, although I had no idea if it was any good. We ate it on her front porch, where it was a little cooler. If she noticed I didn't sweat, she didn't mention it.

"Things better with Jerry?" she asked.

"Better." I nodded. She seemed to have forgotten our conversation from the night before. Perhaps she thought it was all talk, that I really wouldn't have gone through with ending Jerry's existence, or, at least, that's what she wanted to believe because she wanted it so badly. I couldn't be so inhumane. Maybe that's why she still made love to me. Maybe that's why she still let me into her home.

"Will you be staying long?" she asked, and I knew from the way her voice ended on a high note that she was hoping I'd say yes.

"Hard to say," I answered. "It will still take a lot of work."

She stretched out her leg, let it rest on my lap. "You can stay as long as you like, you know."

"Thanks, I appreciate that."

"Then—" she paused "maybe afterwards, we can go somewhere together."

I pushed her leg away. "I don't think that's such a good idea. You hardly know me."

"I know more than you think," she said. She came over to me, sat down on my lap. It was then I realized that she knew, or at least guessed, my nature. "But how?" I asked.

She shrugged. "I just did. I got a funny feeling in the pit of my stomach when you walked into Dino's. I had the same feeling with Jerry, when I first saw him coming out of the Piggly Wiggly with his mom after the funeral."

"It's a rare gift," I said.

She put her arms around my neck. "It's made me closer to you," she said. "So, you see, I know about you, and I don't care. Together, we can start new lives, be in love again."

"But I'm not alive," I replied. "And I can't love."

"My husband was alive, he was capable of love, and that was a disaster." She gestured to the run-down house, a symbol of her life. "You at least choose to be the way you are. In some ways, that's more real."

"It's just a façade."

"It's more than that. You have that spark. That's why you help people like Jerry, isn't it? To nurture yourself? To keep something in you alive?"

In the distance, a train whistle blew three times. I said, "My existence, it's not for you. Better you stay here."

She laughed. "Easy for you to say. You don't have to live in this town."

"Leave then. Make your own life, but not with me." I rose, pushing her from my lap, but grabbing her hand so she wouldn't fall. I started to walk away, Denise calling after me. It was better for her this way. There were other towns, other men, better than the ones here, better than me. She deserved the real thing.

I was almost to my car when a pickup truck pulled up beside me and three guys piled out of the back, another two got out form the front. Dark shadows against the deep blue night. In an instant, they were on me, grabbing my wrists and ankles. I struggled, but there were too many of them.

They pulled me to the ground on the shoulder of the road. I felt something being wrapped around my legs, a heavy chain. I lay bound, still as a rod, while they kicked me and spat on me. I did not shout, did not beg or cry. I had done that before. This time, I would not give them the satisfaction.

They scrambled back into the truck. I lifted my head, saw that the other end of the chain which had my legs was tied to the rear bumper. One of the men in the bed pounded on the roof of the cab. The engine revved, and the truck sped off. I was dragged across the gravel, onto the blacktop, down the road, over the tracks. I could hear them whooping and hollering, their stereo blaring. I could feel my legs being pulled from their sockets, although it didn't hurt like it should.

After a few miles, they stopped the truck, unhooked the chain from the back, and sped off. One of them shouted something, I couldn't tell if it was "nigger" or "nightmare." I lay in the middle of the road, stone still. Let them think they did real damage so that they wouldn't come back.

When I was sure they were gone, I rose, brushed myself off. I could feel the scrapes, the bruises, the cuts, but if I had been alive, I wouldn't have been able to walk. I probably would have been dead all over again. I started back to my car. The next day, I would return to Jerry's, continue my work. Tomorrow, they'd see me walking through town. I'd say hello with a wide, white Uncle Tom grin as if nothing had happened. In some ways I was grateful. Denise was right; what I did for those like Jerry fed me, gave me a surge of elation. Something like this fed me as well. It was almost as good.

"WE WERE AT THE RANCH, JUST OFF 29," Jerry's voice was emotionless, monotone, but at least he was talking. "Jonesy, Karen, Lois, and me. Lois and I had been dating two years. We were drinking and dancing and having a great time. The Lonesome Doves were playing that night. Well, come closing time, Jonesy was pretty lit. Too lit to drive, I knew, but I didn't say anything. I should've but I didn't. I was more than a little drunk myself, and I didn't want to cramp his style in front of Karen. So, we got into his Grand Am, and me and Lois started making it in the back seat. I didn't take any notice of Jonesy's driving. Next thing I knew, Karen screamed. We swerved. Everything went dark. I woke up in my own bed. I was me, but I wasn't me, you know?"

"Do you know what happened to the others in the car?" I stood, leaning against the windowsill, blocking Jerry's view out his bedroom window.

"Mom told me Jonesy and Karen didn't make it. Lois has had three operations. She's still in the hospital."

"Have you thought about seeing her?"

"I wouldn't know what to say, how to act. I can't seem to feel anymore. I'm all dead inside. Mom, she looks at me like I'm a stranger."

"Would you like to be her son again?"

"I don't see how I can."

"I can teach you," I said. "What to say, when to say it, how to hold your head. I can show you how to act like a person again."

"Will that make me alive?" he asked. "Will I ever be the same?"

I shook my head. "No. Don't fool yourself into believing that. But with practice and work, you'll seem like it to everyone else. Be the boyfriend, maybe even the husband, of Lois' dreams. Be the son your mother knows and loves. You may not feel inside. I may just be going through the motions, but it will seem real to everyone else. I won't lie to you, though. It will be hard work, and it will take time. Both for you and me. I'll only help if you're willing to make the commitment."

He was silent a moment, as if thinking. "Do I have a choice?" he asked.

I reached into my bag, pulled out the syringe. "It's painless. But then again, for you, almost everything is."

He took the syringe, pulled off the cap that covered the needle. He poked himself several times in the arm, careful never to go too far or press the plunger. I understood what he was doing. He was seeing what effect the threat of being destroyed would have on him. He was trying to feel.

He handed the syringe back to me and went to the window. His mother was walking from the clothesline to the house, laundry basket in hand. "Helping me, like you said. It will be good enough," he said.

I nodded. I stepped up to him, put my hand out, smiled. He looked at it, puzzled.

"You shake it," I explained, pushing it towards him, "and you look me in the eyes. And when I smile, you smile back."

He took my hand, looked at me, smiled a little too broadly. That was okay. He'd learn.

"I'll see you tomorrow afternoon, after your chores are through. We'll begin for real then." I headed out of the bedroom and into the kitchen. Mrs. Terrence was waiting for me. She had made a sandwich, ham and cheese, with fried potatoes on the side. I sat down to eat. She smiled at me. I smiled back. It was the correct response.

Acknowledgments

Gratefully acknowledged are the following publication, where stories appeared in earlier forms:

"The Fae Sing," *Aurora Wolf*

"Old Rocker," *Liquid Imagination*

"Panel by Panel," (Originally published as "My Life in Pictures"), *Not One of Us*

"The Resurrectionists," *Dark Recesses*

"One Block at a Time," *Triptych Tales*

"Beneath the Linden Tree," *Daikaijuzine*

"The Shape of Things," *Alienskin*

"The Lonely Box," *Underland Archana*

"How to Protect Your Child" (Originally Published as "A Son in Winter"), *Short Story Me!*

"Dress Up," *Nanobison*

"Standing Still," *Theme of Absence*

"The Correct Response," *Tales of the Unanticipated*

This book wouldn't have been possible without the help of so many others. I'd like to thank all the readers with both the Pen & Ink Writer's Group and Karma Weasels. I especially want to thank Steve Fox for encouraging me to submit my stories for this collection in the first place.

I would also like to thank everyone at Cornerstone Press, notably publisher Dr. Ross Tangedal, editor Ellie Atkinson, sales and media directors Sophie McPherson and Ava Willett, and the rest of the press staff. Their diligence, patience and hard work have made this collection better than anything I could have imagined.

My family has been an invaluable source of encouragement. My brothers and sisters have always been there for me. My children have shown me, and sometimes straight out told me, how children should talk, feel and act. My ex-wife, Dianne, remains a true friend and source of support.

Lastly, I must mention Steve Athanases, the teacher who initially saw that I had a talent worth nurturing, and wrote "WOW!" across that first poem I wrote junior year of high school and started me on this long and winding path of storytelling.

MANFRED GABRIEL's short stories have appeared in over two dozen publications, most recently in *Modern Magic*, *December Tales II*, and *Epic Echoes*. He lives and writes in western Wisconsin, where yes, hot air balloons do occasionally brush up against the trees.